THE INCREDIBLE HONEYMOON

The Earl of Lemsford stared at his prospective son-in-law in undisguised horror.

"I think Your Grace has made a mistake!"

"Not at all," replied the young Duke, "it was actually your second daughter I had in mind—Lady Antonia . . ."

"Antonia?"

"Of course," the Duke continued, "if you do not wish to give your consent to such a union . . ."

"My dear fellow, I'm not saying you cannot marry Antonia," the Earl said quickly, "I merely thought you would prefer my elder daughter. No matter . . . Ah, Antonia, may I introduce His Grace the Duke of Doncaster. The Duke has asked for your hand in marriage."

"I am indeed honoured, Your Grace," Antonia said in a quiet voice. But the Duke was certain that she winked at him.

BARBARA CARTLAND

Bantam Books by Barbara Cartland
Ask your bookseller for the books you have missed

Barbara Cartland

The Incredible Honeymoon

BANTAM BOOKS · LONDON
TORONTO · NEW YORK

THE INCREDIBLE HONEYMOON
A Bantam Book | September 1976

ISBN 0-553-02806-5

Published simultaneously in the United States and Canada.

Bantam Books are published by Bantam Books, Inc. Its trade-mark, consisting of the words "Bantam Books" and the por-trayal of a bantam, is registered in the United States Patent Office and in other countries. Marca Registrada. Bantam Books, Inc., 666 Fifth Avenue, New York, New York 10019.

PRINTED IN THE UNITED STATES OF AMERICA

Author's Note

While the main characters in this novel are fictitious, the facts regarding the Siege of Paris are all correct. The British Ambassador and the British Consul did leave on September 19, an action which provoked considerable anger, both at home and among the British left in Paris.

Balloons carrying despatches and mail took off at the rate of two or three a week. Sixty-five balloons actually left Paris during the Siege, of which only four fell into enemy hands.

The Siege dragged on. Early in October, Parisians began to eat horse-flesh; from mid-November the Zoo provided exotic menus. No animal was exempt.

A journalist colleague of Henri Labouchere—the details about him are factual—wrote during the first days of January—"I have now dined off camel, antelope, dog, donkey, mule, and elephant."

There was a notable price between "brewery" rats and sewer rats and there were 380 cases of smallpox in January. The final capitulation of Paris to the Prussians took place on January 27, 1871, but no Prussian troops were to enter Paris for the duration of the armistice which was to last until February 19.

The terms were harsh: Paris was to pay an indemnity of two hundred million francs, surrender the perimeter forts to the Prussians, and throw the rampart guns into the moats.

Henri Labouchere, having lived through the Siege and the terrible aftermath, returned home to British political life. It was, however, observed by his friends that the Siege had markedly aged him.

Chapter One

1870

"I have something very important to say to you!"

The Marchioness of Northaw spoke with an intonation in her voice which made the Duke of Doncaster, who was putting the finishing touches to his cravat, pay attention.

He was looking in the mirror and by moving his head slightly to one side he could see the Marchioness lying against the tumbled pillows of the bed, her naked body as beautiful and iridescent as a pearl.

With her fair hair falling over her white shoulders she was in fact the most beautiful woman to whom the Duke had ever made love, and without exception the most passionate.

"What is it?" he asked.

"You will have to be married, Athol!"

The Duke was startled into immobility; then he turned round to say with laughter in his voice:

"Surely this is hardly an appropriate moment to speak of the holy bonds?"

"I am serious, Athol, and this is in fact a very appropriate moment."

"Are you suggesting that we should be married?" the Duke enquired incredulously.

"No, of course not!" the Marchioness replied, "although I assure you, Athol, I would like it above all things! But George would never give me a divorce.

1

There has never been a public scandal in the Northaw family."

"Then what is worrying you?" the Duke asked.

There was no doubt she was worried: there was a distinct pucker on the perfection of her oval brow and the blue eyes were clouded with anxiety.

There was a pause, then the Marchioness said:

"The Queen knows about us!"

"That is impossible!"

"Nothing is impossible where the Queen is concerned, as you well know. There is always some spiteful old woman, doubtless one of your relatives or George's, to whisper poison in her ears."

"What makes you think Her Majesty is suspicious?" the Duke asked slowly.

"She more or less told me so," the Marchioness replied.

The Duke sat down on the end of the bed he had so recently vacated.

The Marchioness pushed herself up a little higher against the lace-edged pillows, regardless of the fact that the only covering down to her small waist was her long, silken, golden hair.

She looked, the Duke thought, like the sun rising at dawn, but for the moment her beauty left him cold. He was too concentrated on what she had just told him.

"It was last night at the Ball," the Marchioness explained. "When we had finished dancing and I had returned to the dais, the Queen beckoned me. She was smiling and I sat down beside her, thinking she was in a pleasant mood."

She paused to say viciously:

"I should have remembered that when she smiles she is always at her most dangerous!"

"Go on with what happened," the Duke ordered.

Despite the fact that he had not yet put on his coat, he looked exceedingly elegant in his fine lawn shirt, embroidered with his monogram surmounted with a coronet, and with his white collar showing against his grey cravat.

He was athletically built with square shoulders and narrow hips. As the Marchioness's eyes rested on him, the pucker between her eyes vanished, and as if she could not help herself she put out her hand towards him.

He ignored it.

"Go on," he said, "I want to hear exactly what Her Majesty said."

The Marchioness drew in her breath.

"She said in that ingenuous manner which hides her Machiavellian brain: 'I think, Marchioness, we must find the Duke of Doncaster a wife!'

" 'A wife, Ma'am?' I exclaimed.

" 'It is time he was married,' the Queen said. 'Handsome unattached Dukes are such a disturbing influence.' "

The Marchioness made a little gesture.

"You can realise, Athol, I was too astounded for the moment to be able to reply. There was no mistaking the innuendo in the Queen's voice. Then she went on: 'You must use your influence, and of course your tact, Marchioness. They are two qualities I greatly admire and which I always seek in my Ladies of the Bedchamber.' "

The Marchioness ceased speaking and the Duke was silent too. Then after a moment she continued:

"You know how much I want to be appointed to the Royal Household! It would be such a snub to all my sour-faced viper-tongued sisters-in-law who have always looked at me down their noses and openly deprecated the fact that George married anyone so young and unimportant."

"You will certainly enliven the gloom at Windsor!" the Duke remarked.

"And Buckingham Palace," the Marchioness said quickly. "You forget the Queen is now coming to London far more than she used to, and naturally I shall try to persuade her to do so as much as possible."

"You really think that in such circumstances we could go on seeing each other?" the Duke asked.

"If you were married—yes!" the Marchioness answered. "But not otherwise. She would prevent it somehow—you can be certain of that. And I am quite sure she will not appoint me unless you are married or at least engaged."

The Duke rose to his feet to walk to the window and look out at the trees in the Square outside.

"So I am to be sacrificed to make a Roman Holiday!" he said, and there was a sharp note in his voice.

"You have to marry sometime, Athol. You must have an heir."

"I am well aware of that," the Duke replied, "but there is no hurry."

"You are thirty and it is time you settled down," the Marchioness said.

"And do you imagine that is what I would do?" he asked.

Once again there was a note of cynical amusement in his voice.

"I cannot give you up!" the Marchioness cried. "I cannot! I have never loved anyone as I love you, Athol! As you well know, you excite me as no other man has ever been able to do."

"Quite a number have tried!" the Duke remarked.

"That was because I was so unhappy. George is only interested in Greek urns, ancient history, and Italian Masters."

The Marchioness paused before she said passionately:

"I want to live today. I am not interested in the past nor particularly in the future for that matter. I just want you to go on making love to me, for us to be together as we are now."

"I thought we had been so careful," the Duke said beneath his breath, as if he spoke to himself.

"How can anyone be careful in London?" the Marchioness asked. "There are servants who talk; there are people on the other side of the Square who watch the carriages stopping outside my door; and there are all those women who look at you with hungry eyes and who loathe me because you are no longer interested in them!"

The Duke's lips twisted a little at the corners.

"You flatter me, Clarice!"

"It is the truth—you know it is the truth!" the Marchioness retorted. "If I have had a few lovers, it is nothing to the legions of women you have left with broken hearts."

The Duke made an irritated sound and walked back to the mirror to continue adjusting his cravat.

The Marchioness sensed he was annoyed and remembered that he always disliked any reference to his many love-affairs.

But she told herself she was so sure of him that nothing could disrupt the wild ecstasy they found in each other's company.

Never, she told herself, had she known a more passionate or more ardent lover.

Never had she been more determined that, whatever the Queen might say, whatever the difficulties that lay ahead, she would not give him up.

"Listen, Athol," she said now as he stood with his back to her, "I have a solution—the perfect solution to the problem."

"If it involves my giving my name to some nit-witted girl, I am not interested."

"Oh, Athol, do be sensible! You have to marry sooner or later, and I cannot lose the opportunity of becoming a member of the Royal Household. It will give me an aura of respectability I have never had before!"

"I would not be surprised if you found it a millstone round your neck!" the Duke remarked.

"It will make everything so easy," the Marchioness said pleadingly. "We shall be able to see each other not only surreptitiously in London but also in the country."

"How do you reason that out?"

"Because where it has been difficult for you to come

to the Hall or for me to visit you at Doncaster Park,
there will be a thousand excuses if you have a wife and
I am friendly with her."

"And you really think any wife would accept you as
her friend as well as mine?"

"Of course she will! Especially the girl I have already chosen for you."

The Duke turned round sharply.

"This is too much, Clarice! If you really think I
would allow you to choose my wife, you are very much
mistaken!"

"Do not be so stupid, Athol!" the Marchioness retorted. "You know as well as I do that you never come
into contact with young girls. When are you likely even
to meet one moving between White's Club and this
house, between Newmarket and Epsom, Ascot, or your
Hunting-Lodge in Leicestershire?"

"I must admit there are few débutantes to be found
in such surroundings," the Duke agreed.

"Then you must leave it to me," the Marchioness
said, "and actually, not only can I provide you with a
complacent, well-bred, unobtrusive wife, but also with
the extra acres of land that you always wanted at the
end of The Chase at Doncaster Park."

"You mean Lemsford's land?" the Duke enquired.

"Exactly! When you marry Felicity Wyndham you
ask as her dowry the three hundred or so fine acres of
her father's Estate, which adjoins your own."

"Really, Clarice, you seem to have it all tied up!"
the Duke expostulated. "But may I point out that I
have never seen this Wyndham girl? In fact I had no
idea that she even existed!"

"Why should you?" the Marchioness enquired. "But
I am well aware that you have always coveted that particular acreage which would make the ground where
you exercise your horses, as you have so often said
yourself, into a miniature race-course."

That was true and the Duke could not gainsay it.

It had in the past proved a constant irritant that the
Earl of Lemsford, his next-door neighbour in Hertford-

shire, should own a piece of land which had once been part of his family Estate but had been lost at cards by his great-grandfather.

As if she realised her advantage in the discussion, the Marchioness went on:

"The Earl is, I know, extremely hard up and looking for a rich son-in-law. Felicity Wyndham is very pretty, in fact if you do not compare her with me, outstandingly so!"

"I imagine by that remark that she is fair-haired and blue-eyed," the Duke said.

"Exactly!" the Marchioness agreed. "And what could be more proper for a Duchess? Fair-haired women always show off jewellery so much better than brunettes."

She gave a little sigh.

"Oh, Athol, you must know how much it will hurt me to see another woman at your side and see her glittering with the Doncaster diamonds, which are far more magnificent than anything poor George ever possessed!"

Her lips tightened for a moment before she went on:

"But, darling, neither of us can afford a scandal, even if you were prepared to run away with me, which I doubt."

"If I asked you, would you come?" the Duke asked with a cynical twist to his lips.

The Marchioness was still for a moment, then she said:

"I have often asked myself that question, and I think, if I am truthful, the answer is no. How could I bear to live abroad, to be ostracised and cut by everyone we know? You would be all right. The man always is. It is the woman who suffers in a *cause célèbre*."

The Duke knew this was the truth.

"Well, Clarice," he said, "you have been very persuasive, but naturally I must have time to think over this extraordinary proposition."

"There is no time to think," the Marchioness said sharply. "You know as well as I do that if there is a vacancy among the Ladies of the Bedchamber, there will be a dozen old harridans manoeuvring for themselves, their daughters, their nieces—or anyone rather than me!"

"Are you really suggesting," the Duke asked, "that I should make up my mind on such an important subject now—at this moment?"

"If you love me you will not hesitate," the Marchioness said. "But you know, Athol, it would be an inexpressible agony if we have to say good-bye to each other. I do not think I could bear it."

There was a break in the soft voice.

"We could go on as we are now," the Duke suggested.

"And do you suppose someone would not tell the Queen?" the Marchioness asked. "How can we meet knowing we are being spied on, that everything we do and perhaps everything we say is repeated back to that Old Spider spinning webs in her Sitting-Room at Windsor?"

"All I will promise you," the Duke said firmly, "is that I will think seriously about it."

He took his coat from a chair as he spoke, put it on, and pulled it firmly into position over his square shoulders.

He glanced down at the dressing-table to see if there was anything he had forgotten. Then he walked across the room where the Marchioness lay watching him from the bed.

She looked up at him, her eyes very blue against her white skin.

"I do matter to you?"

"You know you do," the Duke replied. "But love is one thing, Clarice, marriage is another!"

"It is love which counts," the Marchioness said softly.

The Duke took her hand and raised it to his lips.

"Thank you, Clarice, for making me very happy."

His lips lingered a moment against the softness of her skin. Then her fingers tightened on his and she drew him towards her.

"Good-bye, my darling, wonderful, magnificent lover!" she whispered.

She raised her lips as she spoke towards his.

Just for a moment he hesitated, then as he bent forward her arms were round his neck, pulling him down upon her. . . .

He tried to resist but it was too late.

Her lips, wildly passionate, held him captive, and he felt the fire that was never far from the surface rising within him to match the fire which was burning in her.

He had the feeling that he was surrendering himself not only to her violent, exotic desire but also at the same time to the loss of his freedom.

But for the moment it was not important!

*   *   *

The Earl of Lemsford slit open one by one the letters which lay beside his place at the breakfast-table.

The Butler had provided him with a silver letter-opener engraved with the Lemsford coat-of-arms.

That it needed cleaning passed unnoticed by the Countess, who, seated at the other end of the table, was admonishing her daughter Felicity for having torn her gown the night before.

"I cannot think why you are not more careful, Felicity. If you danced the waltz more sedately these accidents would not happen."

"I could not help the man standing on the train of my gown, Mama. I said when I fitted it that it was too long."

"It looked so elegant when you walked into the room," the Countess said.

Her eyes rested on her elder daughter and the irritation which had expressed itself in lines round her mouth seemed to fade.

Felicity Wyndham was in fact very pretty. She had china-blue eyes, fair hair, and a skin which was invariably referred to as "strawberries and cream."

She had a beguiling way of looking at her parents that made it hard for them to deny her anything, and the Countess was already calculating how she could persuade her husband to give her enough money to buy Felicity another gown.

On the other side of the table, Antonia sat unnoticed.

She had no wish to draw attention to herself; for if she did she was quite certain she would be sent on an errand or made to listen to what was being said while her food grew cold.

Accordingly, she applied herself to eating her eggs and bacon without glancing up, until her father gave such a loud exclamation that it seemed to reverberate round the Dining-Room.

"Good God!"

"What is it, Edward?" his wife enquired.

"When did this letter arrive?" the Earl asked.

He picked up the envelope and without waiting for a reply went on:

"It was delivered by hand. It has not been sent by post. Why the devil was it not brought to me at once?"

"Really, Edward, not in front of the girls!" his wife admonished.

"Do you know who this is from?" the Earl enquired.

"No, of course not! How should I?"

"It is from Doncaster!"

The Earl paused, an expectant look on his face, as if he were a conjurer about to produce an unexpected rabbit from a hat.

"Doncaster?" the Countess repeated. "Do you mean the Duke of Doncaster?"

"Of course I mean the Duke!" her husband snapped. "There is only one Doncaster as far as I am concerned! Our neighbour in Hertfordshire, Emily, who has never invited me inside his house since he inherited!"

The Earl spoke with a bitterness which showed that this was an old grievance.

"Well, he has written to you now," the Countess said. "What does he want?"

The Earl stared down at the letter as if he could not believe his eyes. Then he said slowly:

"His Grace asks, Emily, if he can call on me at three o'clock tomorrow afternoon. He informs me that he thinks it would be to our mutual advantage to have a closer association between our two families than has hitherto existed, and he hopes that he may have the pleasure of making the acquaintance of my daughter!"

The Duke's voice died away and he realised that the three people seated at the table were staring at him with their mouths open, looking not unlike three goldfish in a bowl.

The Countess recovered first.

"I do not believe it!" she said. "Give me the letter, Edward. You must have made a mistake!"

"There is no mistake," the Earl replied, "unless my eyesight is at fault!"

He threw the letter across the table to the Countess. It landed in a dish of marmalade, from which it was hastily retrieved.

The Countess held it in her hands, staring at it in the same fascinated manner that her husband had done.

"Why does the Duke say that he wishes to . . . meet me?" Felicity asked in a frightened voice.

The Countess looked at her daughter and there was a sudden light in her eyes that had not been there before.

"You will be a Duchess, Felicity!" she said. "Think of it—the Duchess of Doncaster! I never thought—I never dreamt that we should ever aspire so high!"

"I would have wagered it being one hundred to one against Doncaster," the Earl remarked.

"But why? Why me?" Felicity enquired.

"He must have seen you somewhere. He must have fallen in love with you!" the Countess said ecstatically.

"There is nothing like that about it," the Earl remarked sharply. "There is some other reason, and I will find out what it is before I am very much older!"

"Are you inferring, Edward, that the Duke would wish to marry Felicity for any other reason except that he wants her to be his wife?"

"I am not saying, after reading that letter, that he does not wish her to be his wife," Sir Edward replied. "I am merely saying that he has not fallen in love like some beardless boy. Doncaster is a man, Emily, and a man who by all accounts has more women fawning round him than he has horses in his stables. If he wants to marry Felicity—and I find it hard to believe it— then there is something behind it, you can bet your shirt on it!"

"Really, Edward, I do dislike those vulgar racing expressions!" the Countess retorted. "If the Duke does wish to marry Felicity, then we should go down on our knees and thank God for such a miracle, without trying to find ulterior motives for his proposal!"

The Earl rose to his feet.

"Where are you going?" the Countess enquired.

"I intend to answer this letter," the Earl replied, "then I am going to White's. If old Beddington is there, which he will be, he will tell me the latest scandal and what Doncaster has been up to lately."

"You will not mention that the Duke is coming here tomorrow?" the Countess said quickly. "We may be mistaken. He may have very different intentions."

"I am not a fool, Emily," the Earl said. "If there is any blabbing to be done, it will not be done by me."

He went from the room, and as the door shut sharply behind him the three women left at the table looked at one another.

"I can hardly believe it!" the Countess said.

"But I do not want to marry the Duke, Mama!" Felicity said in a small voice.

Her mother did not appear to hear her as she stared down at the Duke's letter as if the words written on the thick vellum paper must be printed indelibly on her mind.

Felicity would have spoken again, when she received a sharp kick on the ankle which made her wince.

She looked across the table and saw her sister frowning at her warningly and the words she was about to say died on her lips.

"We must go upstairs at once and decide what you will wear tomorrow afternoon when the Duke calls," the Countess said after a moment. "I think it will have to be the pale blue: it is so becoming with your eyes. But then, so is the white with the turquoise ribbons threaded through it."

She gave a sound of exasperation.

"There is no time to buy you anything new, so it will have to be one or the other! Oh dear, I do hope you have not made them dirty!"

Rising from the table, the Countess bustled away and her daughters followed her.

Only as they reached the door of Felicity's bed-room did she turn and say sharply:

"There is no reason for you to hang about, Antonia. I am sure you have plenty to do, and if you have not, I will find you something. You know that you have to help tidy the Sitting-Rooms. You cannot expect Janet to do everything!"

"No, of course not, Mama," Antonia replied.

She moved away as she spoke, giving Felicity a warning glance and at the same time a touch on her arm which told her sister she would be back later.

There were always innumerable jobs in the house for Antonia. They were understaffed and she was invariably expected to fill in for deficiencies in housemaids, lady's-maids, and even footmen.

It was Antonia who made the Sitting-Rooms presentable, who cut the sandwiches for tea when they entertained, who pressed and mended her mother's and Felicity's gowns, and who was sent on messages from the top of the house to the bottom.

But she was used to it and it did not unduly perturb her.

This morning, however, she wished that she could be in the bed-room with Felicity while the Countess was choosing her gown for tomorrow, simply because she was afraid that Felicity would betray herself.

To learn that she had not done so was a relief, when finally an hour later Antonia entered Felicity's bed-room to find her alone.

As soon as she saw her sister, Felicity ran across the

room to put her arms round Antonia and burst into tears.

"What am I to do? Oh, Antonia, what am I to do? I cannot marry this Duke . . . you know I cannot!"

Antonia held her sister close, then she said:

"Come and sit down, Felicity, and let us talk about it. You can see what it meant to Mama and Papa."

"I know! I know!" Felicity sobbed. "They are not going to listen to me . . . whatever I say . . . but I love Harry. You know . . . I love him, Antonia!"

"Yes, dearest, but Harry is not a Duke."

"He loves me," Felicity said, "and I promised I would marry him as soon as he can approach Papa."

Antonia gave a little sigh as she wondered how she could possibly explain to Felicity that, whatever Harry Stanford might say now, the Earl was not going to listen to him.

The son of the Squire who owned an attractive Manor-House on a very small Estate, Felicity and Antonia had known Harry ever since they were small children.

They had met him at parties and, as they had grown older, out hunting. It was difficult for Antonia to remember when first she realised he had fallen in love with Felicity and she with him.

They had all known that it was impossible for Harry to approach the Earl when Felicity was only seventeen, and being only three years older himself he had certainly not enough money to keep a wife.

His circumstances were not much better at the moment.

As he was an only child, he would inherit, on his father's death, his Estate, such as it was, and there was also a bachelor uncle who had always promised to make him his heir.

Harry had wished to ask the Earl's permission to marry Felicity before they came to London for the Season, but Antonia had advised them against it.

"Papa and Mama have been saving up for years so

that Felicity can have a proper Season in London and be presented at Court," she said. "As you know, it should have happened last year just before Felicity was eighteen. But when Mama's father died we were all plunged into mourning, and so Felicity's début had to be postponed."

"Supposing she meets someone else?" Harry had asked despondently.

"I think it unlikely," Antonia replied, "that she will ever love anyone but you."

It was strange, seeing that Antonia was a year younger than her sister, that everyone referred their problems and troubles to her, and that was another role she played in the household. Even her mother was more inclined to ask her advice rather than Felicity's.

"What am I to do?" Harry Stanford had enquired helplessly.

"Wait until the Season is over," Antonia advised. "Then when we are back in the country you can approach Papa. I am sure he will be more amenable then."

What Antonia really meant was that there was a chance for him unless Felicity had had a very advantageous offer of marriage.

She privately thought it unlikely.

Although Felicity was extremely pretty and men fluttered round her in the proverbial manner of moths round a flame, they thought twice before proposing marriage to a girl who had no dowry and only the possibility of five hundred acres of not particularly productive Hertfordshire land when her father died.

That, of course, was if the Estate was not sold and divided equally between his two daughters, which Antonia always doubted.

But while Felicity had received much flattery and never lacked partners at a Ball, up to date there had been no positive approach to her father and no suggestion of anything more permanent than a flirtation in the garden.

Now, out of the blue, the Duke of Doncaster had
appeared, and Antonia knew that it put away any hopes
Harry Stanford might have of becoming Felicity's husband.

"I want to marry Harry! I love him! I will never love
anyone else!" Felicity was saying.

When she raised her face, looking lovely despite the
tears which ran down her cheeks, Antonia felt desperately sorry for her.

"I think you have to face facts, dearest," she said.
"Papa would never permit you to marry Harry when
you could be a Duchess."

"I have no wish to be a Duchess," Felicity said. "I
just wish to live quietly with Harry. I have much enjoyed the Season and the Balls, Antonia, but I kept
thinking of him and how much more fun it would all
have been at home."

Antonia knew this was the truth, and she thought
apprehensively that there was no doubt that Felicity
would be unhappy living a life of pomp and circum-
stance.

She also knew a great deal more about the Duke than
anyone else in the family did; she could in fact have
answered her father's queries about the Duke's motives
for his proposal very nearly as competently as the old
crony he was going to consult at the Club.

As their Estates marched with each other, the Duke
owning some ten-thousand acres, Antonia had always
been extremely curious, not so much about him as about
his horses.

The one love of her life was horse-flesh, and while
she had ridden since she was a small child, she had always been allotted the worst and oldest horses to ride,
which neither her father nor her sister required.

Nevertheless, it was Antonia who managed by some
magic of her own to enthuse the laziest and sometimes
the most aged beast into action, and who was invariably
in front of the field out hunting and in at the kill.

But it was impossible for her not to realise almost
since she could walk that just over the boundary hedge

were the most magnificent thoroughbreds that any lover
of horses could desire.

What was known as The Chase was a long gallop
which ended abruptly at the Earl of Lemsford's boundary.

The part of Hertfordshire where Doncaster Park and
The Towers, in the Earl's Estate, were situated was un-
dulating, wooded, and a large part of it was cultivated.

But only a mile from the Duke's Mansion, The Chase
provided a flat, perfect stretch of Park-land which had
once extended for another quarter of a mile into what
was now owned by the Earl of Lemsford.

Ives, the Duke's head groom who had lived in Hertfordshire all his life, soon became aware that there was
always a small girl staring wistfully over the fence as he
and the stable-lads took the horses for their morning
gallop.

As the small girl grew older, her friendship with the
elderly man meant a great deal to both of them.

He even came to say himself:

"Ye knows as much about horses, M'Lady, as Oi
knows meself!"

"I wish that was true," Antonia would answer. "Now
tell me about the day the Duke's horse won the Derby."

There is no man who does not enjoy an attentive
audience and Ives was no exception.

He had no children of his own and the tales he used
to relate to Antonia would hold her spell-bound, her eyes
fixed flatteringly upon him until he would describe so
vividly the races he had attended that she felt as though
she had been there herself.

It was only a question of time before Antonia was introduced to other members of the Duke's household.

Mrs. Mellish, the Housekeeper, who often found that
time lay heavy on her hands, was prepared to guide the
very appreciative young lady from next door round the
great Mansion.

But it was the Curator, Mr. Lowry, who taught her
the most,

The Earl had no appreciation of the arts and if his ancestors had ever possessed pictures or furniture of any value they had long since been sold.

Only rather badly executed portraits of the Wyndhams remained, because they were unsalable rather than because they were appreciated.

But Doncaster Park was filled with pictures, furniture, *objets d'art,* and treasures which had been collected over the centuries, each one contributed by a member of the Casterton family and having a history that Antonia found absorbing.

Because Mr. Lowry taught her far more than did the inadequate Governesses provided by the Earl, Antonia after she was fifteen spent more time at Doncaster Park than she did in the School-Room at The Towers.

The Governesses, realising that she counted the least in the family, were not concerned by her absence and concentrated on trying to instil the very meagre knowledge they themselves possessed into Felicity's mind.

Because she was very pretty they decided, like her parents, that she would not require many talents and education was therefore not important.

There was only one thing that the Countess did insist upon, and that was that both her daughters should speak fluent French.

"All ladies of good breeding can speak French," she said loftily, "and as people are going abroad more and more, just in the same way as foreigners come here, it is essential that you should both speak with a Parisian accent."

The fact that she and her husband were invited to a large party given when Louis Napoleon and the Empress Eugénie came to England in 1857 accentuated her determination that her daughters should not be lacking in this accomplishment even if they possessed few others.

Antonia found French easy and she liked the old retired *Mademoiselle* who came to The Towers from St. Albans twice a week to give her and Felicity lessons.

"I cannot remember all those tiresome verbs," Felicity would cry despairingly.

But Antonia had not only mastered the verbs but was soon chattering away to *Mademoiselle,* finding out many things she wanted to know about France and especially Paris.

Unlike the other Governesses who concentrated on Felicity and ignored Antonia, *Mademoiselle* reversed the procedure.

Because Antonia had a natural ear, she taught her and let Felicity sit silent, deep in her own thoughts, which certainly did not concern French.

"There are two things anyway I know a lot about," Antonia told herself once. "The first is horses, and that is thanks to Ives, and the second is French, thanks to *Mademoiselle!*"

Mr. Lowry found some books at Doncaster Park which satisfied both interests, and because they seldom conversed with their younger daughter the Earl and Countess would have been surprised if they had known how knowledgeable she was, or how widely and extensively she read.

As soon as the Earl could do so he dispensed with the services of the Governesses, thereby saving their meagre salary and keep. Despite the fact that the family was in mourning, Felicity was considered now to be grown up and no longer in need of lessons.

That Antonia was a year younger did not perturb either her father or her mother.

The Countess had already stated categorically that she was not going to have two unmarried daughters "out" at the same time.

She said it in a way which made Antonia sure that she thought it unlikely that her younger daughter would ever get married, and even if she did, it would be to no-one of any importance.

As Antonia regarded herself in the mirror she was not surprised.

Unlike Felicity's, her hair was dark, or very nearly

so. It was not, unfortunately, the jet-black tresses beloved by romantic novelists.

Instead it was an indecisive colour, dark enough to give her dark eye-lashes for her grey-green eyes, but not, she thought, enough to make her skin seem the dazzling white that was so fashionable amongst the young Ladies of Fashion.

"It is shadowy," Antonia said to herself disparagingly. "I wish it were red and my eyes a vivid green—then perhaps someone would notice me!"

It was difficult to look outstanding in the clothes she wore, as they were always those which had been discarded by Felicity, and Antonia knew that the colours which suited Felicity's Dresden-china appearance did nothing to flatter her.

But she was too inexperienced and not interested enough to worry about it.

The only thing that did concern her about clothes was her riding-habit.

While she was not allowed to be fitted as Felicity was by a London tailor, the local man in St. Albans did his best because he liked Antonia and she was so pleasant to him.

She took him a pot of honey because his wife had a persistent cough during the winter, and she talked to him about his children.

She was also considerate when he told her that he had not finished her habit because a fox-hunting gentleman was wanting a pair of breeches who was a good customer and a better payer than the Earl.

"I understand, Mr. Jenkins," Antonia said. "But do try to make me have a small waist and see that the jacket fits really well over the shoulders. I am not worrying about myself so much, but it does show off to advantage the horse I am riding."

"That's true, M'Lady," Mr. Jenkins replied.

Antonia found later that he had spent far more hours on her habit than the small amount of money he received for it justified.

What she did not tell Mr. Jenkins, and what she certainly would not have told her father, was that Ives occasionally permitted her to ride the Duke's horses.

She exercised them with him and the stable-boys and found it impossible to say how thrilled and delighted she was at the opportunity.

"It's a real pity, M'Lady," Ives remarked, "that ye can't ride one of these horses out hunting. Then ye'd give 'em something to talk about!"

"I would indeed!" Antonia agreed. "And think how jealous everyone would be! But they would be certain to tell His Grace and then I would be back on the other side of the boundary where you first found me."

This was a joke between them and Ives laughed.

"That's true, M'Lady. Oi've never forgotten how ye looked with yer big eyes peeping at me from between the branches. It annoyed me at first to think ye were spying on us, until Oi realised it was a real interest ye were showing and we got to know each other."

"We did indeed, Ives," Antonia replied, "and it was the luckiest day of my life."

She used to think she could put up with any disagreeableness at home so long as she could get away and be with Ives and the horses.

It compensated her for the unhappiness she often felt at being unwanted.

When she had been very young and she had first realised that she was a constant irritation to her father because she was not a boy, she had cried bitterly because she could not please him by changing her sex.

As she had grown older and learnt from the Nurses and other servants that the Countess in bringing her into the world had suffered so badly that the Doctors said it was impossible for her to have another child, Antonia began to understand how deeply disappointed her father had been.

"The Earl was convinced he would have a son," the old Nanny told her. "The cot and everything else was decorated with blue ribbons, and he was to be called

Anthony, which is a family name, as you well know."

"So that is why I was called Antonia!"

"Nobody had thought you would be a girl. Then as they expected both you and your mother to die, you were Christened a few hours after you were born.

" 'What name is she to be given?' the Doctor asked me.

" 'The baby was to have been called Anthony, Sir,' I replied, seeing that your poor mother was incapable of speech.

" 'Then it had better be Antonia,' he remarked."

Antonia had tried to make up for her unavoidable deficiency by being a son to her father.

She would ask if she could go out shooting with him. She would beg him to take her riding.

But she soon realised that even to look at her annoyed him and reminded him of the son he would never have. So instead she kept out of his way, and soon no-one in the house worried about her unless she was late for meals.

Then she was severely punished.

So she soon learnt to tear herself away from Ives however absorbed she was in his stories. Or to run into the house after she had been riding, giving herself just time enough to change into a suitable gown and walk breathlessly but demurely into the Dining-Room before the Earl was aware of her absence.

Now, Antonia thought as Felicity sobbed against her shoulder, the attractive and undoubtedly, if she ever met him, irresistible Duke was likely to become her brother-in-law.

It was impossible for her, spending so much time at Doncaster Park, not to hear the servants gossiping, and it was not only the servants who talked of their Master but also her mother's friends.

Because the Duke was the most important and certainly the most interesting person in that part of Hertfordshire, he was an endless topic of conversation to everyone in the vicinity of Doncaster Park.

The fact that he never concerned himself with local people when he was in residence did not stop their tongues wagging or their learning in one way or another of his various love-affairs.

Antonia was so insignificant and made herself so quiet and unobtrusive that it was easy for the ladies talking round the tea-table to forget that she was there.

She would hand round the sandwiches and cakes, pass the cups of tea, and then retire into a corner of the Drawing-Room, out of sight, out of mind, but listening with rapt attention to everything that was said when it concerned the Duke.

She knew when one love-affair ended, she knew when the next one began.

She heard of jealous husbands who found it difficult to prove what they suspected, she learnt over and over again of women who proclaimed to all and sundry that their hearts were broken and that life would never be the same once the Duke had loved but left them.

It was as fascinating as some of the romantic novels that had been lent to her, not by Mr. Lowry, who would not have allowed anything of that sort in the Library, but by the Governesses who passed the long dreary hours when they were alone in the School-Room reading of the love they were never likely to experience in their own lives.

Antonia thought the books a lot of nonsense, until she found that some of the episodes in them were much more true to the Duke's life than ever she had imagined they could be.

"I wonder what it is that makes women go wild where he is concerned," she asked herself.

She looked at the pictures of him hanging on the walls of Doncaster Park.

Although they showed an exceedingly handsome and fine-looking man, she felt there was something missing, something she could not explain to herself but which she was sure was not portrayed by the artists.

She had, it was true, seen the Duke when he was

riding on The Chase, which he always did when he was staying at Doncaster Park.

But on Ives's instructions she kept well out of sight, merely peering at him over the boundary fence and thinking how magnificently he rode, so that he did in fact seem to be part of his horse.

He was usually at a gallop when he passed her, so that it was impossible to see his face closely or the expression in his eyes.

Antonia had always wished to meet him and now it seemed she was likely to do so, not tomorrow, for she was quite certain that her mother and father would not allow her to be present when he called to see Felicity, but later when the engagement was announced.

At the thought of an engagement Antonia's arms tightened round Felicity.

She knew how this was going to hurt her sister and she could not help thinking from what she knew of the Duke that Felicity would be unable to cope with him.

She was a sweet, gentle girl, but as Antonia knew only too well, extremely stupid in many ways and very vulnerable if she was not cosseted, fussed over, and loved.

Would the Duke do that? And was it likely that he would want to?

"What shall I do, Antonia? What shall I do?" Felicity sobbed despairingly.

And Antonia found herself thinking of the Marchioness of Northaw.

Chapter Two

The Duke was finishing his breakfast, which had been a substantial one, when the Butler came to his side to say respectfully:

"Excuse me, Your Grace, but Lady Antonia Wyndham has called to see you."

The Duke was surprised into thinking that he must have been mistaken.

"Lady Antonia Wyndham?" he repeated.

"Yes, Your Grace."

"At this hour?"

"Yes, Your Grace."

The Duke looked even more astonished.

"Has she come alone?"

"No, Your Grace. She has a maid with her who is waiting in the Hall. I have shown Her Ladyship into the Library."

The Duke put down his knife and fork and lifted a cup of coffee to his lips.

He always ate a large meal at breakfast-time, believing it to be important to his health. He preferred coffee to any other beverage and was never known to touch alcohol however much he had indulged the night before.

He had made it a rule, and he organised his life on rules that he made for himself, that he would always rise early.

When he was in London he rode in the Row before it became fashionably crowded with the Ladies of Quality who wished to gossip with their friends and the Pretty

25

Horse Breakers who were intent on showing off their mounts.

To call on him at half past seven in the morning was something which had not yet been attempted by any lady, however persistent she might be in pursuing him.

As he finished his coffee and took a last glance at *The Times,* which he had propped up in front of him on a silver stand, the Duke was wondering what this early visit could mean.

How was it possible that the Earl of Lemsford's daughter should not know that it was extremely unconventional, not to say reprehensible, for a lady to call at a bachelor establishment?

He was also irritated to think that she would make him late for his ride.

Already the stallion that he had ordered from the stables would be waiting for him outside the front door, and undoubtedly any delay on the part of his Master would make it hard for the stable-boys to hold the animal.

The Duke therefore walked purposefully and without a welcoming expression on his face into the Library.

As he entered the room a small figure turned from the window and at his first glance he realised that the girl who had come to see him was not in the least what he had expected.

He was quite sure that the Marchioness had described her as having fair hair and blue eyes.

Had she not said that was the right colouring for a Duchess and would become the Doncaster diamonds?

Then as he recalled the conversation he remembered that in fact the Marchioness had said that the girl she had chosen for his wife was called Felicity.

The Duke looked at Antonia and was not impressed.

For one thing, she was badly dressed in an extremely ill-fitting gown of faded blue gabardine, and her bonnet, which was small and inexpensively trimmed, seemed to obscure most of her hair.

The eyes she raised to him, however, were very large in her pointed face and he saw that she was nervous.

"I hope Your Grace will . . . pardon me for calling at such an . . . early hour."

"It is certainly an original way of our becoming acquainted," the Duke replied. "Am I correct in thinking it is your sister I am to meet this afternoon?"

"Yes," Antonia replied, "my sister, Felicity."

"I thought I had not been mistaken in the name."

Then with a gesture of his hand the Duke said:

"Will you not sit down, Lady Antonia, and tell me to what I owe this unexpected visit?"

Antonia sat down on the edge of a comfortable sofa and regarded her host with wide eyes.

He was far better-looking, she thought, than he had appeared when she had seen him riding on The Chase, and now that they were at close quarters she realised what it was the artists had omitted to include in their portraits of him.

It was a raffish, perhaps cynical, but certainly mocking look which they had omitted, whilst striving to portray his clear-cut features, broad brow, and deep-set eyes.

"He is much more attractive than they portrayed him!" Antonia told herself.

The Duke had seated himself opposite her in a wing-back armchair.

He crossed his legs and she saw that his riding-boots were exquisitely polished and wondered if it would be impertinent to ask him what was used on them.

Then she remembered that Ives could find this out for her and she determined she would ask him to do so when she next went to Doncaster Park.

"I am waiting, Lady Antonia," the Duke said with just a note of impatience in his voice.

"I . . . I think," Antonia said a little hesitatingly, "and I . . . hope you will not think it an impertinent guess, that when you call on my father this afternoon you will ask for my sister's hand in . . . marriage."

There was a noticeable silence before the Duke replied:

"That was my intention."

"Then would you . . . mind very much asking for . . . me instead?"

The Duke sat bolt upright in surprise. Then, as he realised after a perceptible pause that he had not been mistaken in what she had said, he replied:

"I think you should explain yourself a little more clearly. I must admit I am wholly at a loss to understand what is happening or why you have come here with such a suggestion."

"It is quite easy to understand, Your Grace," Antonia replied. "My sister, Felicity, is in love with someone else!"

The Duke was aware of a sensation of relief.

"In which case it is quite obvious that she will refuse my proposal and there is in fact no point in my calling on your father this afternoon."

He thought to himself as he spoke that this set him free from carrying out the Marchioness's plan, and she could hardly blame him if the girl she had chosen to be his wife would not accept him.

"Papa is expecting you," Antonia replied, "and is of course extremely excited, and so is Mama, at the thought of having you as a son-in-law."

"I can hardly marry your sister if she does not want me," the Duke said with a smile on his lips.

"You do not suppose she would be allowed to say so?" Antonia asked scornfully. "As it happens, neither Papa nor Mama have the slightest idea that she is in love. Harry, the man in question, has not up to now been able to speak to Papa."

The Duke looked at Antonia, and a little uncertainly she went on:

"You cannot be unaware that Felicity would be forced to marry you whatever her feelings are?"

"That is ridiculous!"

Even as the Duke spoke he knew that what this strange girl was saying was undoubtedly the truth.

He was too well versed in the social world not to know that as the most eligible bachelor in the country every match-making Mama would wecome him as a son-in-law.

Any girl he chose as his wife would be compelled to marry him willy-nilly, whatever her secret feelings might be on the matter.

It had, however, never crossed his mind in this instance that there would be any opposition where Felicity Wyndham was concerned.

He had not really thought of her as a person, but just as a complacent, compliant young woman who would be overwhelmingly grateful that he should condescend to offer for her.

"I am afraid I am not pretty like Felicity," Antonia said, breaking in on his thoughts, "but as it does not really matter to you what your bride looks like so long as she fulfils her duties and produces an heir, I think you will find one Wyndham sister is very like another."

The Duke rose to his feet.

"Who told you it did not matter what my wife looked like?" he asked sharply.

Antonia hesitated for a moment and he had the idea that she was choosing her words with care before she replied:

"It is obvious, Your Grace, is it not? You have not seen Felicity and she has never seen you . . . but you are prepared to offer her marriage and everybody has been saying for a . . . long while that you need an . . . heir."

"I cannot help thinking this is the most extraordinary conversation to have with a young girl," the Duke said. "Does your father know you are here?"

"No, of course not!" Antonia replied. "Mama thinks I am attending early Communion with Janet, who is our maid. It was my only possible excuse for escaping from the house when there is so much to do in preparation for your call this afternoon."

"You really wish me to consider your extraordinary proposal seriously?"

"Why not?" Antonia enquired. "Felicity has cried all night and is making herself ill at the thought of marrying you. I have to do something to help her, and apart from my looks I would make you a better wife than she would."

There was an irrepressible smile at the corners of the Duke's lips as he asked:

"How can you be certain of that?"

"I would make no demands on you, for one thing," Antonia replied, "and I would be quite happy staying in the country when you were in London. In fact I would be very content to be at Doncaster Park."

"And you really think you would like to marry me?" the Duke asked.

His question surprised Antonia into telling the truth.

"If I could ride your horses," she answered, "I would marry . . ."

She checked herself quickly.

She had been about to say: "the devil himself!" but realised it would have sounded extremely rude. So she substituted a little lamely:

". . . the owner of them!"

The Duke had not missed her hesitation before the sentence was finished.

"You sound as if you know my horses," he said. "I suppose, since you live next door, you have seen them?"

"I have watched them on The Chase," Antonia said. "They are magnificent! Especially Red Duster. I think you have a winner there!"

"I think so too," the Duke agreed, "but until a horse has won his first race, one can never be sure how he will shape when he is actually on a course."

"Ives is confident that he will prove to be as good as, if not better than his sire," Antonia said.

The Duke looked at her speculatively.

"I have a feeling, Lady Antonia, that you have in fact a more intimate knowledge of my horses than you have gained just by looking over the boundary that separates our lands."

He saw the colour come into her face as Antonia realised she had more or less betrayed herself.

"I am . . . very interested in . . . horses," she said not very convincingly.

"Especially mine!" the Duke said. "So much so that you are prepared to marry me for them!"

"It is not exactly like that," Antonia said a little shyly. "Any girl would be deeply honoured at the idea of being your wife, but Your Grace must admit it is a little difficult to be sure of what a man is like until one has at least met him—or for that matter a horse until one has ridden him!"

She knew the last sentence was impertinent, but she could not help adding it.

"And of course you know my horses better than you know me!" the Duke remarked.

There was a mocking note in his voice which she did not miss.

"I know you must think it very strange for me to come here and make the suggestion that I have. Mama would be absolutely horrified! But there was really nothing else I could do to save Felicity."

Again Antonia realised that her choice of words was not particularly flattering and she added quickly:

"If she were not already in love I feel sure Felicity would have been delighted by your proposal, as any other girl in her position would be."

"And if, as you say, she is in love," the Duke said, "then the only alternative is for me to marry you."

"I really would do my best to make you a good wife," Antonia said gravely. "It is not only that I know a little about your horses, I am also very interested in Doncaster Park and all the treasures it contains. Mr. Lowry has told me about your ancestors and I can understand why you are very proud of them."

The Duke did not speak and after a moment Antonia went on:

"I have not been well educated, except that I have read a lot."

"No doubt the books in my Library?" the Duke remarked.

Antonia realised he was more perceptive than she had imagined he would be.

"Quite a number, Your Grace," she admitted truthfully, then added quickly:

"I hope you will not be angry with Mr. Lowry because he lent me your books. I have known him for years, ever since I was quite small, and he realised how very inadequate my Governesses were to teach me the things I wanted to know!"

The Duke did not speak and she went on:

"Because I asked so many questions he would often lend me a book on the subject. I was very careful of them!"

Antonia looked at the Duke anxiously.

"I think I must commend Mr. Lowry for adding to your knowledge," he said after a moment, "and I am glad that my books, which I often think are sadly wasted in that large Library, should have been put to some really useful purpose."

Antonia gave a little sigh of relief.

"Thank you, Your Grace. I should be very distressed if Mr. Lowry found himself in trouble on my account."

"You were telling me about your education," the Duke prompted.

Antonia gave him a smile that transformed her pale face.

"I am afraid," she said, "that what I know about horses, the knowledge I have acquired from your books, and a capacity for speaking French comprise my entire repertoire."

"You have no other talents?" he enquired.

"None that I know of! I never have time to paint in water-colours or embroider cushion-covers."

She gave a little sigh.

"I suppose that shows I am not very feminine, but then I ought to have been a boy!"

The Duke raised his eye-brows and she explained:

"Papa longed for a son and was quite certain that I would be one. I was to have been Christened 'Anthony.' "

"I see," the Duke said. "So to make up for it you have become what is known as a 'tom-boy.' "

He looked as he spoke at the unbecoming bonnet on her hair, which he saw was not dressed in a fashionable manner.

He also glanced at her ill-fitting gown, which had been made for Felicity and now had been altered, although not at all skilfully.

He had not expected a young girl to have the elegance, the *chic,* or the sophistication of women like the Marchioness, whom he had found so desirable and indeed so irresistible.

But vaguely at the back of his mind he had thought of a débutante in spotless white with wide innocent blue eyes, golden hair, and looking something like the angels in the picture-books his mother had read to him as a child.

Antonia did not look in the least like an angel, and in fact her appearance was not at all what he had envisaged in his wife.

As if she realised what he was thinking, Antonia said a little nervously:

"I am sure I could look . . . better than I do now if I could wear a new gown which had been chosen especially for me."

"You mean . . . " the Duke began.

"I am the younger sister, Your Grace!"

Antonia could not help smiling at his perplexity.

What did the Duke know about being poor? she thought, of striving to make ends meet, wondering where the money would come from to pay the bills that poured in day after day?

He had always lived in the lap of luxury. He had always been a rich man with great possessions, the owner of a proud title.

"How can he possibly understand," she asked herself scathingly, "what ordinary people have to put up with in their lives?"

Because she suddenly felt annoyed and at the same time slightly deflated by his scrutiny, Antonia rose to her feet.

"I think, Your Grace, I should go now," she said. "My father will be waiting to greet you at three o'clock this afternoon. If you feel you could not contemplate having me as your wife, I shall quite understand. Felicity is very lovely and perhaps in time she will grow fond of you."

"You appear to have set me a problem, Lady Antonia," the Duke said. "My choice appears to be between a young woman who, if she is truthful, will hate the sight of me, and another who is enamoured of my horses and not in the least of me as a man!"

He spoke sarcastically and Antonia answered him without thinking:

"It might be very inconvenient for Your Grace to have a wife who was much interested in you for yourself."

"What are you suggesting by that?" the Duke enquired, and now there was an icy note in his voice that had not been there previously.

"Only that in the sort of marriage you envisage, Your Grace . . . an arranged marriage . . . which is to bring an . . . advantage to both parties, it would be best if you had . . . other interests, and that your wife should have . . . some too!"

There was a pregnant silence. Then the Duke said:

"And where you are concerned it would be my horses?"

"Exactly!" Antonia said.

She had the feeling that he was annoyed, if not positively angry, at what she had suggested and thought despairingly that she had messed up the interview: now there would be no chance of his doing what she wished.

She was certain that when he came to see the Earl in the afternoon he would ask for Felicity's hand and not hers.

"I have tried and failed!" Antonia told herself. "I can do no more."

She curtseyed very politely and as she rose said:

"I must thank Your Grace for listening to me. I deeply regret that I have delayed you from going riding."

"I shall think with great care about all you have said to me, Lady Antonia," the Duke said, "and whatever my decision, I hope I shall have the pleasure of seeing you this afternoon."

"That, I can assure you, is very unlikely," Antonia replied, "unless of course you ask for me."

She gave him a quick glance and he thought her eyes had a sparkle of defiance in them.

Then before he could reach the door she had opened it herself and was hurrying across the Hall to where her maid was waiting.

The Butler led them out and the Duke stood staring with an expression which was almost one of stupefaction, until the door closed behind them.

"Good God!" he muttered to himself.

He knew that he was more surprised by Antonia's appearance and what she had said to him than by anything that had happened in his life for a very long time.

'The whole situation is absurd—utterly absurd!' he thought as he rode towards the Park.

He avoided the Row where he was certain to meet a number of acquaintances and galloped in the less-fashionable part on the other side of the Serpentine.

Although after an hour's exercise he undoubtedly felt better in himself, he still found it impossible to decide his future.

Everything had seemed comparatively simple when Clarice had persuaded him that Felicity Wyndham was exactly the type of wife he required and beguiled him into writing to the Earl of Lemsford.

It was true, the Duke thought, that at the back of his mind he had assumed that any woman he honoured would be content to live in the country except on special occasions.

Although the Marchioness had said it would be easier for them to see each other when they were both in Hertfordshire, he had the uncomfortable feeling that there might be prying eyes and just as many gossiping tongues in the country as there were in London.

Now for the first time the full impact of what he was about to do seemed to strike him like a blow.

Could he really contemplate spending a lifetime with a woman in whom he had no interest and who, even if she did not interfere with his love-affairs, might prove an intolerable burden in other ways?

"What would we talk about?" the Duke asked himself as he slowed the stallion, now not so frisky, down to a trot.

If he married Antonia, he told himself, it would undoubtedly be about horses.

He had not missed the light in her eyes when she spoke of them or the excitement in her voice.

The Duke was not used to women showing interest in other subjects when he was present.

If their faces lit up, it was when they looked at *him!* If their voices deepened with excitement, it was because *he* excited them!

Antonia certainly did not look like the type of woman he had envisaged as bearing his name.

Yet there was something about her which made it difficult for him to dismiss her as completely unattractive.

Her clothes were lamentable, but at least she was conscious of their deficiencies and she might, as another woman would put it, "pay for dressing."

"The whole thing is ridiculous!" the Duke told himself. "How can I possibly marry a girl who comes to my house early in the morning and offers herself to me in place of her sister?"

Then he thought it was really no more extraordinary than marrying the sister he had never met.

He realised that neither the Marchioness nor he himself had for one moment considered the possibility that the girl they had chosen for such an enviable position might positively dislike the idea and in fact be in love with somebody else.

"I will call the whole thing off," the Duke decided. "I will send a note to the Earl—tell him I have made a mistake—that unfortunately circumstances prevent me from calling on him and I have no desire to meet his daughter!"

He knew even as he spoke the words to himself that to do so would be to insult the Earl gratuitously and unforgivably. Moreover, it would involve him in explaining to the Marchioness why he could not do what she had asked of him.

She had set her heart on becoming a Lady of the Bedchamber, and the Duke knew that the Queen would not have been speaking idly when she had implied it was more or less a condition of the appointment that he should find himself a wife.

"Damnit!" the Duke ejaculated. "Royalty has no right to interfere with one's private life."

But even as he spoke he knew that in the Society in which they moved, Royalty was always interfering.

If there were rules and restrictions as regards Buckingham Palace, there were always innumerable difficulties and problems arising for those who were close friends of the Prince of Wales.

The Duke had only to enter Marlborough House and be alone with the Heir to the Throne to find himself involved in situations that required him to strain every intellectual faculty to find a solution.

"You are a good fellow, Athol! I cannot think what I would do without you," the Prince had said not once but a dozen times in the last year.

And the Duke knew that at least he had certainly earned the Prince's gratitude.

In February he had been deeply involved when His Royal Highness had been subpoenaed to appear in the divorce case Sir Charles Mordant brought against his wife.

Twelve letters from the Prince to Lady Mordant, who was by now in a lunatic asylum, were read out in Court.

Although they were innocuous and the Prince was completely exonerated of having any part in the break-up of the marriage, a whirlwind of public condemnation arose.

The Duke, like most of the Prince's friends, had a hard time defending him.

He had vowed then that he would take care never to find himself in a similar position, which the Queen described as being "painful and lowering."

But marriage!

He was back with his own problem again.

It had already kept him awake, tossing and turning for two nights before he finally had written to the Earl of Lemsford, and felt that the die was cast.

He realised it was time for him to return home to change after his ride.

He had a meeting to attend in the House of Lords at eleven o'clock and he would be late if he did not hurry.

He felt a sudden reluctance to leave the Park until he had made up his mind one way or the other.

"Shall I marry the girl or shall I somehow get out of the mess in which I find myself?" he asked himself aloud.

His horse pricked his ears at the sound of his voice, and quickened his speed, and, as the Duke touched him with his spur, broke into a gallop.

It might not solve anything, but at least he felt better because he was travelling speedily.

*   *   *

"What did he say? What happened?" Felicity asked.

Antonia had only just returned home to be in time for breakfast at half past eight.

When Felicity had looked at her across the table with questioning eyes, she had been unable to give her an encouraging smile for the simple reason that she was now sure she had failed in her quest.

The Earl and Countess discussed all through breakfast the Duke's visit in the afternoon, going over and over for the hundredth time what should be said and what the procedure should be.

"You will first see His Grace alone, Edward," the Countess decided. "Then you will send for me, and what we have now to decide is whether I shall bring Felicity in with me or wait until after I have talked with the Duke myself."

Antonia had heard the arguments for and against so many times that she could no longer give it her attention.

Instead she concentrated on deciding exactly what she should say to Felicity.

It would not be fair to raise her hopes. At the same time, to tell her categorically that she had failed would be to precipitate another flood of tears.

And that, Antonia thought, would solve nothing.

Now walking across Felicity's bed-room, Antonia said slowly:

"The answer is, Felicity, I really do not know!"

"What do you mean, you do not know?" Felicity asked frantically. "Will he marry you instead of me? Surely he must have told you if he would!"

"He said he would think about it."

"How can he want me? How can he?" Felicity asked despairingly. "You told him I was in love with somebody else?"

"I made it quite clear. But after all, there is no reason why that should worry him when he is in love with the Marchioness!"

"And if he is, surely it cannot matter to him who he marries, whether it is you or me."

"I more or less said that," Antonia admitted, "but I am not as pretty as you, Felicity! Duchesses should be outstanding and beautiful, as you well know!"

"You certainly look dreadful in that old gown of mine," Felicity said. "What on earth made you wear it?"

"I have nothing else," Antonia said simply. "Your green one is so tight it is almost indecent! And I have had no time to mend the pink one which had burst its seams through sheer old age! After all, you wore it for years before it was handed down to me."

"If there had been time you could have altered one of my new gowns," Felicity said.

"And what do you suppose Mama would have said to that?" Antonia asked.

She realised how distressed her sister was looking and said soothingly:

"It may be all right, Felicity. We must just pray he will think it better to ask for me, since I am willing to marry him, than for you, who cannot bear the idea."

"I will not marry him! I would rather die!" Felicity said dramatically. "I belong to Harry . . . I always have. I could not . . . I would not let another man . . . touch me!"

"I suppose all women feel like that when they are in love," Antonia said as if she was speaking to herself. "But why are men so different? They seem to be able to make love to two or three women at the same time without it perturbing them!"

"That is not love!" Felicity said. "It is something horrid! Harry says that because he loves me he can never even see another woman! They just do not exist where he is concerned!"

Antonia did not answer and Felicity suddenly put her arms round her sister.

"Oh, Antonia, help me, help me!" she cried. "I am so frightened, so terrified that I shall be made to marry this horrible Duke and never see Harry again!"

"I am sure it will be all right," Antonia said soothingly.

At the same time, even to herself her voice sounded uncertain.

*   *   *

The Duke arrived at 29 Chesham Street precisely at three o'clock, and as a concession to the importance of the occasion he travelled in a closed carriage.

It was not a great distance from Berkeley Square to Chesham Street in Belgravia, where the Earl had a small and comparatively inexpensive residence.

The Duke's London carriage, with his crest on the painted panels and the accoutrements of silver, was extremely impressive. His horses were superlative.

The Duke himself was resplendent in a morning-coat which fitted him like a glove, and his striped trousers were in the very latest vogue.

His top-hat which sat on the side of his dark hair had the curled brim which Locke had decreed as the *dernier-cri,* and yet everything about him seemed to have that degree of casualness which only a well-bred Englishman could impart to his clothes.

An ancient Butler escorted the Duke up the twisting staircase to the first floor where the Earl was waiting for him in the Drawing-Room.

It had been the subject of another long controversy as to whether it would be more correct for the Earl to be waiting in the small, rather stuffy Study at the back of the house where he habitually sat.

But the Countess had decided it was not impressive enough and the chairs were so shabby that the Duke could not help noticing them.

The Drawing-Room, however, decorated with fresh flowers, was quite a pleasant room, despite the fact that there was a slight stiffness about it as it was usually kept for Receptions or other occasions when the Countess entertained formally.

"Good afternoon, Your Grace," the Earl said with a bluff heartiness. "I am delighted to meet you. I knew your father, but unfortunately I have not had the pleasure of your acquaintance since you were a boy."

Try as he would, he could not help a slight resentment creeping into the tone of his voice.

"It has been most remiss of me not to have invited you to Doncaster Park," the Duke replied. "But as you must know, I am seldom in residence, being kept in London by my duties at the House of Lords, or finding the Leicestershire packs provide me with better sport than those in Hertfordshire."

"We are not a particularly good hunting county, Your Grace," the Earl admitted. "Nevertheless, we can occasionally get an exceptional day on the southern part of your Estate. The coverts at Harmer Green, for instance, gave us the best run of the Season last December!"

"I heard about it," the Duke remarked.

"I think everybody who was out enjoyed themselves," the Earl said. "I was unfortunately not in at the kill, owing to the fact that I am somewhat of a heavy-weight. I lost my second horse."

"That must have been bad luck," the Duke said lightly, "but I dare say your daughter, Lady Antonia, supplied you with a graphic account of what happened."

"Antonia?" the Earl exclaimed in surprise. "Well, as a matter of fact, she did, Your Grace. She rides well and so of course does my daughter Felicity."

"I am sure both your daughters follow Your Lordship's lead," the Duke said politely.

There was a somewhat uncomfortable silence. Then the Earl ventured:

"You said in your letter, Your Grace, that you had the idea that our families should be more closely associated than they have been in the past. May I ask exactly what you mean by that?"

"I think you must already have a good idea of my intentions," the Duke replied slowly.

"You mean marriage?" the Earl enquired heavily.

"That is what I had in mind," the Duke agreed.

There was no doubt about the look of pleasure in the Earl's face as he said:

"It is of course a suggestion, Your Grace, to which I shall give my whole-hearted consent and support. Although I say it myself, Felicity is a very lovely young woman, I feel sure you would like to meet her. Shall I send for her so that she can join us for a few moments before we go further into this matter?"

Without waiting for the Duke's reply, the Earl moved towards the bell-pull hanging at the side of the mantelpiece.

Only as he reached it did the Duke say quietly:

"It was actually, My Lord, your second daughter I had in mind—Lady Antonia!"

The Earl's expression was ludicrous. His hand dropped to his side.

"Antonia!" he ejaculated. "I think Your Grace has made a mistake!"

The Duke's fingers were playing with his gold watch-chain.

"I think not," he said. "Perhaps I was remiss in not stating clearly in my letter to which of your daughters I desired to pay my addresses. It is in fact Lady Antonia!"

"But—I never envisaged such a thing," the Earl gasped, "neither did my wife. Antonia is the younger and . . ."

He paused and the Duke knew he was trying to find words in which to describe his second child.

"I am sorry if I misled you," the Duke said, "but now that it is quite clear, may I suggest, My Lord, that you ring the bell, as you intended?"

The Earl seemed too bemused to argue.

He pulled the bell. When the Butler, who had obviously been waiting outside the door, appeared he said sharply:

"Ask Her Ladyship to come here immediately, and —alone!"

"Alone, My Lord?"

"That is what I said," the Earl affirmed.

The Butler withdrew and a few moments later the Countess, rustling in silk and wearing almost every jewel she possessed, which were not many, came into the Drawing-Room.

Her face was wreathed in smiles and she held out her hand in a welcoming gesture as she said:

"Your Grace! How delightful to see you here! I have always longed to meet our nearest neighbour in Hertfordshire, and it seems unbelievable that the years have passed by without us becoming acquainted!"

"It does indeed!" the Duke answered. "But now, as His Lordship will tell you, the omissions of the past are to be rectified."

"The Duke wishes to marry Antonia!" the Earl said abruptly.

"Antonia?"

The Countess was no less astonished than her husband had been, but quicker than he, she recovered her poise.

"I think you have made a mistake, my dear Duke. You surely mean Felicity, our elder daughter. She is lovely, so very attractive that I have always been certain she will make a brilliant marriage and make some lucky man extremely happy."

"There is no mistake, Emily," the Earl interposed before the Duke could speak. "His Grace means Antonia!"

"I do not believe it!" the Countess exclaimed. "How can you possibly wish to marry Antonia when you can have Felicity?"

The Duke began to grow somewhat bored with the argument.

"Of course," he said, addressing the Earl, "if you do not wish to give your consent to such a union I shall quite understand. In which case, My Lord, I can only withdraw and ask your forgiveness for taking up so much of your time."

His words could not have caused more consternation than if he had cracked a whip under the Earl's and Countess's noses.

"My dear fellow, I am not saying you cannot marry Antonia if you wish to do so," the Earl said quickly.

"No, indeed!" his wife interrupted. "Of course we should be thrilled and delighted to welcome you as a son-in-law, whichever of our daughters you prefer, but it is just slightly surprising. Antonia is . . ."

The Countess paused for a word.

". . . the younger!" she finished lamely.

"I should like to make Lady Antonia's acquaintance," the Duke said.

"I will fetch her," the Countess answered, and casting a despairing glance at her husband went from the room.

"I am afraid I have been remiss in not offering you any refreshment," the Earl said. "I see there is some wine on the table. Would you have a glass of sherry, Your Grace, or would you prefer port?"

"Neither, thank you," the Duke replied. "I make it a rule never to drink in the afternoon. I find at most dinner-parties, especially those at Marlborough House, one has to drink so much that only the most strenuous exercise will shake it off the next day."

"You are right! Of course you are right!" the Earl agreed. "Indeed it is difficult to refuse a drink when one is in convivial company."

The Duke was thinking of a suitable reply to this rather banal chit-chat when the door opened and the Countess returned, followed by Antonia.

She was wearing the same gown she had been wearing early in the morning.

But without the ugly bonnet she did in fact look more attractive, and as her eyes met those of the Duke he knew she was trying to tell him without words how grateful she was.

As she curtseyed he took her hand and felt her small fingers tighten on his.

"May I introduce my daughter Antonia!" the Earl asked ceremoniously. "Antonia, His Grace the Duke of Doncaster has asked for your hand in marriage! I need not say how fortunate your mother and I consider you to be, and I hope you will be fully appreciative of the honour His Grace has accorded you."

"I am indeed very honoured, Your Grace," Antonia said in a quiet voice.

"I hope I shall make you happy," the Duke said a little stiffly.

"And I hope that I may . . . please you, Your Grace."

"That will be all, Antonia," the Earl said. "His Grace and I have various matters to discuss."

He looked at his wife and added:

"I think, Emily, it would be best if we do so alone."

"Of course, Edward," the Countess agreed meekly. "Good-bye, Your Grace. My husband will, I am sure, invite you to dine with us either this week or next, and I feel sure there will be a great many details of the marriage that we must discuss in the near future."

"Of course, Your Ladyship," the Duke replied.

The Countess curtseyed and the Duke bowed.

Antonia curtseyed.

Only as she turned towards the door and her father could not see her face was the Duke almost certain that she winked at him!

Chapter Three

"Your health, Athol!"

It was the third or fourth time the gentlemen seated round the dining-table had drunk the Duke's health and he fancied that some of them were getting a trifle "foxed."

The dinner had been superlative. The Chef had excelled himself in order to impress the Duke's numerous relations who had accepted his invitation to stay at Doncaster Park for his wedding.

The Duke realised that most of them came with not only a sense of relief that he was doing his duty to the family so that he could produce an heir, but also considerable curiosity.

They had none of them met Antonia: their innumerable suggestions that he should take her to Receptions, dinner-parties, or even Balls in London for the purpose of introducing her to the family had met with no response.

'There will be quite enough for them to talk about tomorrow,' he thought.

As if the idea of his wedding weighed heavily upon him, the Duke made an excuse to the cousin sitting next to him and went from the Dining-Room, aware that most of the party had not noticed his departure.

He walked across the huge marble Hall which in Adam's inimitable manner was decorated with classical sculpture set in alcoves, and ignoring the row of attentive footmen, walked down the front steps.

Reaching the gravel sweep in front of the house, he turned not towards the garden but to the stables.

It was later than he expected it to be. Already the sun had sunk and it was neither light nor dark but twilight, which made the great Mansion look like a Palace in a fairy-tale.

The Duke had meant to arrive at his country home far earlier. He had in fact told Mr. Graham to notify Ives that he would ride over The Chase before dinner.

He had looked forward to doing this, because as the flat-racing Season was nearly over he had decided that he would now concentrate on steeplechasing.

Accordingly, he had instructed Ives to have a number of Grand National fences set out on The Chase, incorporating some of the new land he had just acquired from the Earl of Lemsford.

It was something he had planned to do for some years, and while he had been phenomenally successful on the flat, he felt it was a challenge to see if he could train horses which could prove themselves over steeplechasing courses.

The Grand National Handicap Steeplechase, which had first been run in 1839, took place on the last week in March.

Steeplechases had meant a good old hell-for-leather match race across any naturally fenced country that was available.

The sudden prominence of the Grand Liverpool Steeplechase, as it was called, was due to the fact that it was the first jumping race for a really desirable prize.

Twelve hundred pounds was the purse in 1839.

It was four miles across country mostly heavy ploughed, with twenty-nine jumps in all, fifteen to be negotiated on the first round, fourteen on the second.

Two years ago in 1868 a horse called The Laird had won the race, although he was only fifteen hands high, and he had won it again this year, amid scenes of great enthusiasm.

The Duke was determined that in 1871 his colours would be first past the post!

He had bought a horse called Black Knight which he fancied might be exactly what he required. It was an exceptional animal in appearance, but although he had heard a great deal about its performance he wanted to try Black Knight out himself.

Unfortunately, his plan had gone awry because the Marchioness had exerted every wile that she knew to keep him with her.

Like all women, having persuaded him to marry against his better judgement, she was now bitterly regretting that after tomorrow he would no longer be free.

"How can I bear to think of you on your honeymoon, Athol?" she asked. "And how will you bear three weeks, or will it be more, away from England and me?"

"I shall miss you, Clarice, you know that," the Duke said automatically because it was expected of him.

"Promise that when you are in Paris you will think of me every minute, every moment!"

Her arms went round his neck as she said:

"It will not be your wife who perturbs me and makes me so anxious for you, but those exotic, expensive houris with whom you spent so much of your time and money last year."

There was no chance of the Duke refuting this, even if he had wished to do so, because the Marchioness's lips, fiercely, passionately demanding, prevented him from speaking and anyway there was no need for words.

Later the Duke had extracted himself with difficulty but he was so late in reaching Doncaster Park that dinner had to be put back an hour.

There was only time for him to bathe, change, and greet his numerous relations before they proceeded into the great Baronial Hall which Adam must have designed with just such an occasion as this in mind.

The Castertons were a good-looking lot, the Duke thought, looking down the table.

His aunts, his cousins, and his grandmother all looked, if not magnificent, certainly aristocratic, however old they became.

'Breeding shows itself in bone-structure,' he thought, and was glad that, if he had to marry, his wife should come from an ancient family with a pedigree that was almost the equal of his own.

This, however, was not particularly reassuring when he thought of Antonia as a person rather than a name on a genealogical family-tree.

He had in fact seen practically nothing of her since their engagement had been announced.

Because the Duke felt that the numerous parties that would be given for them jointly and the endless process of being looked over by each other's families would prove intolerable, he had insisted on the marriage taking place far more quickly than his future mother-in-law thought seemly.

There was, however, the excuse that in July everybody would be leaving London.

While for economy's sake the Earl had decided that Antonia should be married in the country at their local Church, the majority of the guests could conveniently come down from London for the ceremony.

"Indecent haste, I call it!" the Countess remarked tartly. "At any rate, it gives me a good excuse to buy you only a small trousseau. Your future husband is rich enough to provide you with anything you need, and what money we have would better be spent on Felicity."

Her mother was being disagreeable, Antonia knew, simply because she could not adjust herself to accepting the fact that the Duke had offered for her rather than for Felicity.

"I cannot understand it!" the Countess said over and over again.

Then finally she found an answer to what perplexed her and the Earl, in the fact that Antonia rode so well.

"He has obviously heard what a 'go-er' she is in the hunting-field," the Earl said.

"Felicity also rides well!" the Countess said, championing her elder daughter as she always did.

"Not as well as Antonia!" the Earl retorted.

Antonia thought during the weeks that preceded the wedding that her mother's dislike expressed itself every time she looked at her and every time she spoke.

She had never made any pretence that Felicity was not her favourite child; but now, Antonia thought, what had been mere indifference where she was concerned had changed into something very much stronger and very hurtful.

There was, however, nothing she could do about it, while Felicity told her over and over again how grateful she was and how both she and Harry would bless her for the rest of their lives.

"As soon as you are married, Harry has decided he will speak to Papa," Felicity said.

"He had better wait until I come back from my honeymoon," Antonia advised. "I will then try to persuade the Duke to say pleasant things about Harry to Papa and Mama and perhaps make them see him in a different light."

"Do you think the Duke would do that?" Felicity asked. "If he would, I am sure Papa would then think Harry was a suitable husband for me."

"I can at least try," Antonia replied.

She wondered as she spoke whether it would be easy to make the Duke do what she wanted and give a helping hand for the second time where Felicity was concerned.

She did not have a chance, however, of approaching him on any subject and she had the idea that he might be relieved that they saw so little of each other.

The Duke was in fact finding his time fully occupied with the Marchioness.

She had been appointed a Lady of the Bedchamber and she thanked him for making it possible by being even more passionate and voluptuous in their moments of intimacy than she had ever been before.

He wondered sometimes how it was possible for a woman who looked almost angelic to be a ferocious tiger when it came to love-making.

As he walked through the high stone archway which led into the stables the Duke was thinking of the Marchioness.

It was almost as if her arms were still clinging to him possessively and her lips were still like a consuming fire against his.

Then he realised the stables were very quiet and knew the stable-boys had retired for the night.

He wished now that he had sent for Ives when he first arrived and explained to the old groom why he could not go round the course as he had planned.

Ives, he knew, would be disappointed.

He had always wanted the Duke to go in for steeplechasing, and now there would be much they had to discuss and a number more horses to be bought before they could really enter a new field in the racing world.

"I am too late," the Duke told himself. "He will have gone to bed."

The horses were all shut up in their stalls for the night.

He was just wondering if he would have a look at Black Knight when he heard the sound of hoofs at the far end of the buildings.

The stables were so extensive that in the dusk it was hard to see clearly what was happening, so that he heard rather than saw two horses being ridden into the stable-yard to enter the stalls at the far end.

The Duke wondered who was out so late, and told himself that perhaps Ives was having a last look at the jumps and wished that he could have been with him.

He walked on and as he drew nearer heard Ives speak, to be answered by a voice he also knew.

"I did it! I did it, Ives! It is the most exciting thing I have ever done in my life!"

"You rode magnificently, M'Lady!" I'ves replied. "But you'd no right to take that untried animal over the jumps, as you well know!"

"But he took them like a bird!" Antonia insisted. "He hesitated just for a moment at the Water-Jump, then he stretched himself out and I swear not a drop of water touched his hoofs!"

"Oi be sure of it, M'Lady, but that jump's too big for a woman!"

"Not for me!" Antonia said proudly.

"Oi don't know what His Grace would say, that Oi don't!"

The Duke stood still outside the stable.

He was aware that Ives and Antonia were unsaddling the horses.

There were two stalls side by side in that particular stable. Ives was rubbing down his mount, making a whistling sound through his teeth that the Duke could remember hearing ever since he was a boy.

"I am quite certain that Black Knight has a chance of winning the Grand National!" Antonia was saying. "You must tell the Duke so."

"And how am Oi to explain to His Grace what a good jumper the horse is?" Ives enquired.

"He should have been here to see for himself," Antonia answered. "We waited until it was nearly dark."

"That be true, M'Lady."

Antonia gave a little sigh.

"Oh, Ives, I wish I were not going away tomorrow. I want to go round the course again not once but a dozen times!"

"Ye'll enjoy yourself abroad, M'Lady. Oi hears as ye be going to France. Them Frenchies have some good horses!"

"Do they? Yes, of course they have! I can see them at the races if His Grace will take me there!"

She sighed again.

"But I shall be counting the days until I can be back, to ride Black Knight for the second time."

"Oi'm only hoping, M'Lady, that His Grace won't consider the horse too strong for ye."

"You know he is not!" Antonia answered. "I do not think there is a horse I cannot handle!"

"That's true, M'Lady. Ye've a way with animals, as

Oi've always told ye. 'Tis something as be born in a person. They either has it or they hasn't!"

There was a silence during which Ives went on whistling through his teeth and the Duke was aware that Antonia too was rubbing down her horse.

"How does the Marchioness of Northaw ride?" She asked in a low voice.

"A Park-rider, M'Lady!" Ives replied disparagingly. "But she's hard on her horses."

"What do you mean by that?" Antonia enquired.

"A groom from Northaw Place were here t'day asking me what Oi uses as a poultice."

"You mean she has spur-galled her horse?" Antonia asked.

"Oi be afraid so, M'Lady, and pretty bad the groom told Oi it were."

"How can these fashionable women be so cruel . . . so insensitive?" Antonia asked furiously. "Seeing the way they ride, only trit-trotting in the Park, there is no reason for them to use the spur, especially the five-pointed rowel, unless it actually gives them pleasure."

Ives did not answer and after a moment Antonia went on, still with a note of anger in her voice:

"Do you remember what Lady Rosalind Lynke did to the horses when she stayed here two years ago?"

"Oi do indeed, M'Lady. We both worked hard on the horses she damaged."

"I have never forgotten it," Antonia said.

"No more have Oi, M'Lady," Ives agreed. "And very helpful ye were. The horses were that nervous and restless from the harsh treatment they'd received that only ye could calm them while Oi applied the poultices."

"I wondered then, and I wonder now," Antonia said reflectively, "what it is that makes those feminine, frilly sort of women so cruel when they are on a horse?"

"Perhaps it be a sense of power, M'Lady. Some women resent a man's superiority, so they takes it out on a dumb beast what can't answer 'em back!"

"I am sure you are right, Ives, and I loathe them for

their cruelty! I swear to you I will never wear a spur, however fashionable it may be, or whoever tells me it is essential to the training of a horse."

She spoke passionately. The Duke turned and retraced his steps towards the house.

As he went he was thinking not of the Marchioness but of Antonia.

* * *

The carriage, decorated behind with two horse-shoes, two old boots, its roof bespeckled with grains of rice, rolled away down the drive.

The Duke sat back against the cushioned seat and thought with a sense of unutterable relief that it was all over!

He had been spared, for which he was extremely relieved, a Wedding-Breakfast which might have lasted interminably, simply because there were too many guests for the Earl to consider entertaining them in such a lavish manner.

Even if they had restricted the Breakfast to relations there would not have been enough accommodation in the Dining-Room at The Towers.

The Church ceremony had therefore been followed by a Reception from which the Duke and his bride could escape in little over an hour.

He had risen in the morning in a depressed mood which he could not shake off, even though he broke his rule of never drinking alcohol at breakfast-time.

The brandy, food though it was, did not seem to alleviate his sense of being pressured into doing something he had no wish to do and also his apprehension about the future.

When he entered the village Church to find it packed to over-flowing and stiflingly hot, he had an almost irresistible impulse to back out of what he told himself was a "mockery of a marriage."

It had been Clarice who had instigated the whole thing, and as he came from the Vestry accompanied by his Best Man and she smiled at him from the fourth pew, he told himself he would willingly strangle her!

She was looking inexpressibly lovely and he thought that it was most insensitive of her to be present at his wedding.

Since she was a near-neighbour, it might indeed have caused comment if she had refused the Earl's invitation.

At the same time, she made him feel uncomfortable and he resented that, just as, he thought savagely, he resented everything else which was happening to him.

There was a stir at the end of the Church and his Best Man whispered:

"The bride has arrived! At least she has not kept you waiting!"

The reason Antonia was on time, the Duke told himself cynically, was not that she was considering his feelings but that she would not wish to keep the horses that were conveying her from her home to the Church waiting in this heat.

Having seen Felicity as she arrived, he could not help asking himself if he could not have been wiser to marry the girl Clarice had originally chosen for him rather than her unimpressive, horsy sister.

Wearing a bridesmaid's gown of pale blue that matched her eyes, and carrying a bouquet of pink roses which echoed the wreath she wore in her fair hair, Felicity looked extremely pretty.

She was in a modest way with her pink and white beauty the counterpart of the Marchioness.

Felicity had curtseyed to him, and as she rose she said in a soft voice which only he could hear:

"Thank You! Your Grace must know how very, very grateful I am."

What other man, the Duke asked himself angrily, in his position and with his reputation, would be thanked by a pretty girl because he had *not* asked her to marry him?

He took a quick glance at Antonia as she came up the aisle on her father's arm and told himself again that he had made a mistake.

It was very difficult to see what Antonia looked like since she wore a Brussels-lace veil over her face.

Her wedding-gown, which had a long train, was carried by two reluctant small children who were being almost forcibly propelled up the aisle by their Nurses.

Behind them, Felicity was the only bridesmaid.

The service was conducted by the Bishop of St. Albans and the local Vicar. The Bishop, besides actually joining the couple in matrimony, gave them an extremely boring address to which the Duke deliberately closed his ears.

Then there was the drive to The Towers under triumphal arches made in the village, with small nosegays of flowers being thrown into the open carriage by the village children.

The Towers, with such a large crowd inside it, seemed even hotter and more oppressive than the Church had been.

By the time Antonia had changed and come downstairs, the Duke was feeling that if he had to wait any longer he would leave alone.

Fortunately—and the Duke had no doubt that she was thinking once again of the horses waiting for them —Antonia was a good deal quicker than most women would have been in the circumstances.

But now they had escaped, the Duke thought with satisfaction, as he brushed the rice from his coat and thought that the pelting of the bride and bridegroom with rice as a symbol of fertility was a pagan custom which should have been done away with a long time ago.

"Do you think we ought to stop and tell the coachman to throw away the horse-shoes and the boots, which I can hear rattling away behind us?" Antonia asked.

"I have had a better idea than that," the Duke replied. "When we are out of the village, and just before we come to the cross-roads, I have ordered my Phaeton to be waiting for us. It may be unconventional, but I thought it would be a quicker way of reaching London."

"And much more pleasant than being cooped up in here for hours," Antonia exclaimed. "It was clever of you to think of it!"

The admiration in her voice mitigated a little of the Duke's irritation that he had been feeling all the morning.

They drove on in silence, and when the carriage came to a stand-still Antonia jumped out eagerly and hurried up the road to where the Phaeton was waiting.

She greeted the grooms in charge, addressing them by name, the Duke noticed, then went to pat the team of four perfectly matched chestnuts.

She talked to the horses as they tried to nuzzle their noses against her and the Duke was aware of an expression on her face that he had not seen before.

"I am glad Rufus is one of the horses taking us to London," she said to Ives. "He has always been my favourite."

"Yes, M'Lady," Ives replied a little uncertainly.

He was embarrassed that Antonia was talking to him in the Duke's presence and showing a knowledge of the horses that he might find hard to explain.

"I think we should be on our way!" the Duke said abruptly. "The guests will soon be leaving your father's house, and it will cause quite a lot of comment if we are seen changing vehicles."

"Yes, of course," Antonia agreed obediently.

The footmen helped her into the Phaeton and a groom sprang up behind them. The Duke set the horses in motion and the four out-riders who were to travel with them to London spread out on either side so as to be clear of the dust.

"This is exciting!" Antonia said. "I was wondering how soon it would be possible for you to drive me in your Phaeton. I was afraid I would have to wait until we came back from our honeymoon."

The Duke glanced down at her and realised that the short satin coat she was wearing over a thin gown was more becoming than anything he had seen her wearing on previous occasions.

Her bonnet also, trimmed with small ostrich-feathers, was fashionable, and he decided that while she did not compare to advantage with her elder sister, she had, perhaps, although he was yet to find them, attractions of her own.

He was relieved to find that she did not chatter all the time they were travelling.

In fact she appeared to be concentrating on the horses, and as they journeyed on towards London the Duke found that the fresh air and the fact that it was not so hot made him feel less constrained and irritable than he had seen before.

After dinner at Doncaster House, where they were to stay the first night of the honeymoon, the Duke in fact felt mellow and almost at peace with the world.

He found that he had enjoyed explaining to Antonia during dinner exactly what his plans were as regards Goodwood Races, which would take place while they were away.

He was also surprised at her knowledge, not only about his own horses bought in the last five years and improving the stud he had inherited from his father out of all recognition, but also how much she knew about the other stables with which they came into opposition on the race-courses.

"How can you have learnt all this?" he asked at one moment.

She had corrected him over the breeding of one of Lord Derby's mares and after a short argument he found that she was right.

"I read the racing-papers," Antonia replied with a smile. "Papa would be horrified if he knew that I did so, because in most of them there are also all sorts of scandalous police reports and slanderous innuendoes about political and social personalities."

The Duke knew only too well to which papers she referred, and he thought they were certainly not the type of reading suitable for a young girl.

He was, however, too interested in what Antonia had to say to find fault.

They moved from the Dining-Room into the Library, although the Duke had suggested they might sit in the Salon upstairs.

"I have learnt that this is your favourite room," Antonia said, "so let us sit here."

"I think the real reason for your choice is that you want to look at my books," the Duke remarked.

"As soon as you have time," Antonia replied, "I want you to show me all the wonderful treasures you have here, which I am told are equally as fine as those at Doncaster Park."

"I have the uncomfortable feeling that you already know more about them than I do," the Duke said.

Antonia did not answer.

He watched her looking round the Library with a faintly amused smile on his lips, being well aware that she was far more interested in her surroundings than in him.

As if she realised what he was thinking, she turned her large grey-green eyes towards him and he had an intuition she was going to say something that was of great importance.

"I have . . . something to ask you," she said.

Now her tone was very different and the gay excitement with which she had been talking all the evening seemed to have vanished.

"What is it?" he asked.

He knew she was feeling for words, but at that moment the door opened and the Butler announced:

"The Marchioness of Northaw, Your Grace!"

The Duke, after a momentary start, rose slowly to his feet.

Antonia rose too as the Marchioness, radiantly beautiful, glittering with jewels, and looking like a fairy on a Christmas-tree, came gliding towards them. The long tulle train of her gown billowed out behind her.

"I am on my way to a Reception at Marlborough

House," she said. "But I had to come in for a second just to give you both my good wishes."

Her words included Antonia, but her blue eyes were fixed on the Duke's and they held a message that only he could understand.

She put her ungloved hand in his and he raised it to his lips.

"It is very gracious of you," he said, "and my wife and I appreciate your expression of goodwill, even at such a late hour!"

It was impossible not to hear the rebuke in his voice, but the Marchioness was quite unperturbed.

"Forgive me for troubling you, Antonia," she said, "but I came out without a handkerchief. I wondered if you would kindly lend me one of yours?"

"Yes, of course," Antonia replied.

She crossed the Library but did not go outside into the Hall, being well aware that the Marchioness's request was only so that she could be rid of her.

Instead she went into the room which adjoined the Library, closing the door behind her.

It was an attractive Salon also overlooking the garden and Antonia had the idea that it was a room which might be allotted to her as the Duke used the Library as his special sanctum.

She thought that the Marchioness must be very sure of the Duke's devotion to have forced herself upon them the first night of his marriage.

Although she knew very little about such things, Antonia was sure that in most cases it would be an embarrassment to a man when his first *tête à tête* with his wife was interrupted by a woman who had been his mistress.

Then she asked herself why she was putting the Marchioness into the past tense.

She was making it very obvious that as far as she was concerned the liaison she had with the Duke would continue as soon as they returned from their honeymoon.

Antonia moved round the Salon looking at the gold snuff-boxes which were arranged on one table, at the Sèvres china which decorated another.

She thought the blue and white porcelain was like the Marchioness and told herself with a little sigh that there was no china which even remotely resembled herself.

It was a disspiriting thought and with a wistful expression she was contemplating the fine bronzes which ornamented the mantelpiece, when the door opened and the Duke came into the room.

"I must apologise, Antonia," he said. "Our uninvited caller had no right to drive you away in that arbitrary manner."

"I realised she wanted to see you . . . alone," Antonia replied, and added in a low voice, "She is very . . . beautiful. I can . . . understand what you . . . feel for her."

The Duke stiffened.

"Who has been talking to you?"

Antonia looked at him in surprise.

"Did you expect me not to . . . know that you . . . love the Marchioness and she . . . loves you?" she enquired. "Everybody knows . . . that!"

"Everybody?" the Duke asked incredulously.

"But of course!" Antonia replied. "And most people . . . I think . . . know that you . . . married because the Queen had more or less . . . commanded you to do so."

The Duke was absolutely astounded.

"How can such a story have got about?" he enquired. "I cannot credit that anything so intimate and secret could be known except by the people concerned."

"Well, Colonel Beddington told Papa," Antonia answered, "and I . . . I also heard it from another . . . source."

"Who told you?" the Duke asked abruptly.

"I would . . . rather not say," Antonia answered.

"I insist on you telling me," he said. "As you have already said so much, I might as well know the rest. Who told you?"

Antonia hesitated for a moment, then as if the hardness of his voice and the look of his eyes compelled her, she replied hesitatingly:

"The Marchioness's . . . lady's-maid is the sister of Mrs. Mellish's daughter-in-law . . . who is . . . married to one of your . . . grooms."

"Good God!"

There was no doubt that the Duke was surprised into being almost speechless.

"Are you telling me," he asked after a moment, "that this is known to all the servants at the Park?"

"Not all of them," Antonia answered. "But they always know what you do . . . and they talk . . . just as the ladies talk in Mama's Drawing-Room . . . except that they are not . . . spiteful about it!"

The Duke looked at her enquiringly and she explained:

"The servants you employ are proud of you! They like to think you are a kind of Don Juan, Sir Lancelot, and Casanova, all . . . rolled into one. They boast about your . . . love-affairs just as they boast about your successes on the race-course. It is a credit to the whole Estate that you should be such a successful . . . lover."

Antonia paused, but as the Duke apparently had nothing to say she went on:

"It is rather different where Mama's . . . friends are concerned. They want to . . . snigger. They do that about everybody . . . but as you are so important and so much more exciting than anyone else . . . naturally everything you do is a special . . . tit-bit with which they regale each other!"

"You absolutely astound me!" the Duke exclaimed.

"I think because you are so . . . attractive and so . . . important," Antonia said after a moment, "you must . . . expect people to be . . . interested in you, and I think too I . . . understand about all the . . . beautiful ladies whom you have loved."

"What do you understand?" the Duke asked.

There was a note in his voice that should have warned Antonia that he was angry, but she was too intent on following the train of her own thoughts to be aware of it.

"I could not think at . . . first," she replied, "why you had to have so many women in your life. Then I thought perhaps it was rather like having a . . . stable. One would not want only one horse, however good, however . . . outstanding. One would want lots of thoroughbreds! Perhaps it is a sort of race in which they all try to reach the . . . winning-post, the prize being your heart!"

She spoke confidently because it was like a story she had told herself.

"I would have never believed any woman of my acquaintance would say anything so vulgar and ill-bred!" the Duke exclaimed angrily.

He did not raise his voice but his tone was icy and like a whip-lash.

For a moment Antonia was still as he glared at her.

Then he saw the colour flood in a crimson tide up her small face until it burnt itself against her eyes.

He saw her tremble, and she turned away from him to stand at the table which held the snuff-boxes, looking down at them with her head bent.

There was something about her slight figure which made him realise that she was very young and very vulnerable. He felt, unaccountably, that he had struck a child.

"I am sorry, Antonia. I should not have spoken to you like that," he said after a moment.

She did not reply and he had the feeling that she was fighting to control her tears.

"What you told me was so utterly surprising," the Duke went on, "that I was quite unnecessarily rude. I have asked you, Antonia, to forgive me."

"I . . . I am . . . sorry," Antonia whispered.

"Will you please turn round?" the Duke asked. "I find it difficult to apologise to your back!"

For a moment he thought she would refuse to do as he asked. Then she turned towards him and he saw there was still a stricken look in her eyes which made him feel ashamed.

"Come and sit down, Antonia," he suggested. "I want to talk to you."

She moved across the room and he found himself thinking she was like a young colt, a little unsteady and unsure of herself, yet ready to trust everyone until she learnt the hard way that not everyone was trustworthy.

Antonia sat down on a sofa and the Duke thought her grey-green eyes were more expressive than any woman's he had ever known.

Before the Duke could speak, Antonia faltered:

"Because I have . . . never been . . . alone with anyone like . . . you, I said what . . . came into my head without . . . thinking. It was very . . . foolish of me . . . I will try not to do it again."

She seemed so humiliated and spoke so humbly that it made her seem even more vulnerable than she had been before.

"I am the one to do the apologising, Antonia," the Duke insisted. "I want you always to say what comes into your head. I want you to be frank with me. If we are to make our marriage work, I think it is essential that there should be no pretence between us. Do you agree?"

Antonia looked down and her eyes were very dark against her cheeks.

"I . . . may say . . . things you do not . . . wish to . . . hear."

"I want to hear about anything and everything that interests you," the Duke said. "I also always want to be told the truth. I made a mistake just now when I snapped at you for telling me just that. My only excuse is that like you I have never been married before!"

He smiled in a manner which much more experienced women than Antonia had found irresistible.

"Is it . . . wrong of me," Antonia asked after a moment, "to speak of the . . . ladies you have . . . loved?"

"It is not wrong," the Duke answered, "but perhaps

a little unusual. However, I would much rather you talked about them than bottle up inside you what you think."

She looked up at him and once again he was reminded of a colt which, having received a blow, was afraid to approach nearer even though it wished to do so.

"Worst of all, I beg you not to take what my Nurse used to call 'umbridge,'" he went on. "It is an emotion to which I have a positive aversion!"

Antonia gave him a wan little smile.

"I will ... try not to ... do that."

"I think that, before we were so unnecessarily interrupted a little while ago, you were about to say something to me," the Duke remarked. "Will you tell me what it was?"

As he spoke he saw the colour burn once again in Antonia's cheeks.

"I ... I think ... perhaps it might make you ... angry."

"If I promise not to be angry but to consider quietly and seriously everything you have to say to me," the Duke asked, "will you tell me what it was you wished to say?"

Antonia turned her head sideways to stare at the empty fireplace.

The Duke noticed for the first time that she had a small straight nose, a firm little chin, and delicately curved lips.

It was only a fleeting impression, before Antonia looked back at him.

"I ... I was going to ask you a ... favour," she said in a low voice, and the Duke realised she had made up her mind to be frank.

"I realise you will think it very ... ignorant of me," she went on, "but I do not know, when a man and woman get ... married, exactly how they have a ... baby. I think perhaps it is because they ... sleep together."

She glanced nervously at the Duke, then looked away again.

"I thought," she continued in a very small voice, "that as you are . . . in love with . . . somebody else, and as we do not . . . know each other very well . . . I might ask you just to . . . wait a little before we . . . had a . . . baby."

As she finished speaking and her voice faltered away into silence, Antonia gripped her fingers together and held her breath.

The Duke rose to his feet and stood with his back to the mantelpiece.

"I am glad you were brave enough to tell me what you were thinking, Antonia," he said after a moment.

"You are . . . not . . . angry?"

"No, of course not!" he replied. "I think in the circumstances you have been extremely sensible in sharing with me what was in your mind."

He paused for a moment, then went on slowly:

"You must try to believe me when I tell you I had no idea that my association with the Marchioness was common knowledge in the country or that it would ever reach your ears."

"Perhaps I . . . should not have . . . told you."

"I am very glad you did," the Duke said. "I am glad too, Antonia, that we can start our life together on a solid foundation. Will you promise me something?"

"What is it?" Antonia enquired.

"That you will keep no secrets from me," the Duke replied. "Not at any rate about important things. However difficult they may appear, I feel somehow we can thrash them out together and find a solution even to the most tricky problem."

He smiled at her again and he saw a little of the nervousness go from her eyes as he went on:

"I think what you have suggested is extremely wise, and I agree that we should get to know each other a great deal better before we do anything so fundamentally important as starting a family."

He saw that Antonia was looking puzzled and after a moment he asked:

"What is troubling you?"

He knew that she was looking at him as if she was wondering whether she dare say what she was thinking. Then she said:

"I have told you I am very ignorant . . . but what I cannot . . . understand is why if . . . when you . . . sleep with me we might . . . have a baby . . . while when you sleep with . . . other ladies, like . . . the Marchioness, they do not . . . have one."

The Duke could not help thinking that this was the most extraordinary conversation he had ever had in his whole life. But he replied very carefully:

"That is one of the questions I would like to answer when we know each other better. Please trust me to explain in the future everything which I am a little reluctant to do tonight."

"Yes . . . of course," Antonia said. "Thank you for being so . . . kind and not being . . . angry with me."

"I will try never to be angry with you again," the Duke said. "But like you I am rather inclined to speak without thinking."

"It is so much . . . easier," Antonia said. "And I have a feeling that if everybody thought before they spoke, there would only be many uncomfortable silences."

"That is true." The Duke smiled. "And now, as we are leaving for Paris tomorrow morning, I suggest, Antonia, that you go to bed. You must be tired after all we have been through today, and it must also have been rather tiring going over the jumps last night!"

Antonia was very still. Then she said in a frightened voice:

"You . . . knew?"

"Yes, I knew. I heard what you had done," the Duke said, "and I can hardly credit it possible. Those jumps, if Ives carried out his instructions correctly, are the same height as those on the Grand National course!"

"It was your new horse," Antonia said. "It was very

. . . presumptuous of me to ride him . . . but we waited until it was nearly dark and you . . . never came."

"It was my loss," the Duke said. "Have you forgotten, Antonia, that my horses are now yours? I distinctly remember saying in the Marriage-Service—'With all my wordly goods I thee endow.' "

There was an unmistakable light in Antonia's eyes.

"I should be very . . . very grateful and . . . honoured if I might . . . share them with . . . you," she said after a moment.

"Then we will share them," the Duke replied. "Just as we will share our thoughts and perhaps, when we get to know each other better, our feelings!"

Chapter Four

The Duke sat in the Café Anglais waiting for Antonia.

He had been surprised, when he had sent his valet to find out at what time she would be ready to leave the house with him, to discover that she had already left.

He had awakened early, as he always did, and while he ate his breakfast he read the French newspapers. The news had been a shock when he and Antonia had arrived at Calais the day before.

They had travelled in great comfort from London to Dover in reserved carriages on the fastest train of the day.

There they had joined the Duke's yacht, which was waiting for them in the harbour, and spent a comfortable night on board, the Channel being as flat as the proverbial mill-pond.

On reaching Calais there were again engaged carriages not only for the Duke and Antonia but also for His Grace's valet and their luggage.

A Courier had gone ahead with instructions from Mr. Graham to have everything booked for the journey and in readiness for when they reached Paris. Owing to his usual genius for organisation, there was not a hitch during the whole journey.

When they arrived it was to find that the house which the Duke had been lent by one of his friends was as charming as he had expected it would be.

Situated just off the Champs Élysées, it was decorated

in Louis XIV style, and when they arrived, Antonia was entranced by the tapestries, the Boucher and Fragonard pictures, and the exquisite Aubusson carpets.

Comfortable though it was, it had, however, been a tiring journey and the Duke had expected Antonia to sleep late.

When he learnt she had left the house by nine o'clock he had thought with a smile that she was not wasting any time.

"Are you very rich?" she had enquired as they were nearing Paris.

It was a question he had been asked before and he replied:

"It depends on what you wish to buy."

"I think you know the answer to that," Antonia said. "Clothes! Even though the few Mama bought for my trousseau are new, I know they are not right for me."

The Duke had looked at what she was wearing and was sure that while the Countess of Lemsford's taste might be impeccable for her elder daughter, where Antonia was concerned there was, as she put it, something wrong.

It might be the fussiness of the frills and furbelows on the very English-styled gown, it might be the pastel shades she had chosen—he was not sure.

He only knew that Antonia did not give the impression of being anything but a rather "frumpy" English bride.

He was, however, too tactful to say so. All he answered, with a smile on his lips, was:

"I am sure you will not bankrupt me! I presume you mean to visit Worth?"

"If you are quite sure you can afford it!"

"I am quite sure," the Duke answered, "and his gowns are superlative. There is no-one from the Empress down to the least-important actress who does not wish to be dressed by Frederick Worth!"

"Perhaps he will not wish to be bothered by me," Antonia said humbly.

Then she exclaimed:

"But of course, I forgot! I am now a Duchess! That must count for something, even in France!"

The Duke had laughed and he wondered without a great deal of curiosity what the great Worth would make of Antonia.

His thoughts of gowns or even of the amusements of Paris were, however, overshadowed by the news he had read in the French newspapers.

It appeared, although he could hardly believe it possible, that France was on the brink of war with Prussia.

Everyone in England had been completely sure that although there was always a certain amount of "sabre-rattling" in Europe, it would come to nothing.

In the spring there had been a spirit of contentment over the whole Continent which had not been seen for many years.

Only two weeks ago the new British Foreign Secretary, Lord Granville, had said blithely to the Duke that there was "not a cloud in the sky."

Peace was everywhere, except, the Duke had learnt, that it was the hottest summer in memory and there were reports of droughts in several parts of France which had the peasants praying for rain.

It was the sort of crisis he was used to in Hertfordshire, and to find the French newspapers filled with news of an incipient war had in fact astounded him.

The Duke was quite certain that the Emperor, whom he had known for many years, in fact since he was exiled in England, had no wish for war. But he was to learn that he was being pushed hard into being aggressive by his heavy-handed Foreign Secretary, the Duc de Graumont.

His hatred of the Prussians was a personal issue because he had never forgiven Bismarck for calling him "the stupidest man in Europe!"

When the Duke, deprived of Antonia's company, had sought an aperitif in the Palais Royal before luncheon, he had met several acquaintances who were only too anxious to discuss the political situation.

"It is the Empress who is determined we shall attack Germany," one of them said. "I have myself heard her declare dramatically as she pointed to the Prince Imperial: 'This child will never reign unless we repair the misfortunes of Sadowa!' "

"I understood the Emperor was not well," the Duke remarked.

"He is not," was the answer. "He has begun to suffer the tortures of the damned from a stone in the bladder."

"In which case I think it extremely unlikely that you will go to war," the Duke replied.

He felt, however, that his friends were not convinced and as he sat in the Café Anglais reading *Le Figaro* he realised that the editorial articles and news items were extremely inflammatory and obviously intended to whip up the flames of bellicosity.

"Thank goodness England will not be involved whatever happens!" the Duke thought to himself.

He was aware that Britain was, if anything, pro-German, as was most of Europe.

The Queen with her German relatives was inevitably more inclined to favour the Prussians than the Emperor Louis Napoleon, of whose personal behaviour and irrepressible Capital she had always disapproved.

"I am sure the whole thing will blow over," the Duke told himself, "and like so many other war-scares will end in nothing but a few diplomatic insults."

He put down the newspaper and looked again at his watch.

He could not help thinking that if there was a danger of keeping the horses waiting rather than himself, Antonia would have been here by now.

The Café Anglais, which was the smartest and the most famous restaurant in Paris, was filling up.

There were a great number of men having luncheon alone because it was near the Bourse, but there were also some very attractive women.

They were all wearing the new gowns which had a suggestion of a bustle and were swept back from the front of the body so that the wearer looked like the figure-head on a ship.

Or, as someone put it more poetically, "like a goddess moving forward against the wind!"

The crinoline had been discarded two years earlier, and although it was still worn in London, in Paris there was not a sign to show it had ever existed.

Instead there was a profusion of beautiful women, so elegant, so *chic,* that the Duke wondered why a man would wish to spend his time and amuse himself in any other Capital.

He had found for himself some years ago how alluring Paris could be.

The only demand was for "pleasure," a criterion set by the Emperor, who never refused the temptation of a new and pretty face.

Louis Napoleon was in fact notorious not only for his love-affairs, but also for his charm and gallantry. Even Queen Victoria had attested to this when she had written:

"With such a man one can never for a moment feel safe!"

It was, however, not safety which men and women sought in Paris, and the great Courtesans of the period had spent more money and established themselves as having more power and fewer morals than in any other period in history.

Immense fortunes passed through the hands of the *demi-mondaines.* Even Egyptian Beys could be ruined in a matter of two weeks.

The Emperor was said to have given the lovely Comtesse de Castiglione a pearl necklace costing 432,000 francs, besides 50,000 a month pin-money, while Lord Hertford, who was reputed to be the meanest man in Paris, had given her a million for the pleasure of one night in which she promised to abandon herself to every known *volupté.*

The Duke had found it all very amusing on his

various visits to Paris, and it did not in fact, he remembered, cost him anything like the large sums expended by his fellow countrymen.

He was not a particularly conceited man, but he did know that the women with whom he had spent his time had welcomed him for himself and were in fact not interested in what he might give them otherwise.

He was just about to draw his watch once again from his waist-coat pocket, when he saw the occupants at other tables near him turn their heads in the direction of the doorway.

The Maître d'Hôtel was speaking to a lady who had just arrived, and although she was some way from the Duke he noticed, as obviously the other gentlemen round him were doing, that she had an exquisite figure.

Dressed in a gown of vivid flamingo pink with touches of white which gave it an indescribable *chic,* it revealed the perfect curves of her breasts and the smallness of her waist before it swept to the ground in a flutter of frills.

As she walked down the restaurant she was the object of every masculine eye, and the Duke could not help ejaculating to himself:

"God! What a figure!"

He was watching the way she moved and it was not until she had almost reached his table that he realised incredulously that the woman he had been admiring was not a stranger and not French—but Antonia!

The Maître d'Hôtel pulled out a chair for her and only then did the Duke rise to his feet, an unconcealed expression of astonishment on his face.

Although he knew that Antonia had large eyes, he had never before realised quite how huge they were or that they filled her small face, which was set on a long, beautifully rounded neck.

Now with her hair swept up in a fashion not yet known in London which gave her a new height, she looked entirely different from the dowdy, insignificant young woman he had brought with him to Paris.

There was something indescribably alluring in the

tiny hat perched forward on the very top of her head
which consisted of little more than ribbons of the same
colour as her gown and a few small white roses.

The angle at which it was set and the shadowy darkness of her hair gave her a piquancy and fascination,
while as to her gown . . .

The Duke glanced again at the perfection of his
wife's body, and wondered if he ought to resent the
fact that it was obvious to every other man in the room
besides himself.

"I did not realise it was you at first," he said.

Antonia's face lit up with a smile.

"That is what I hoped you would say. I do not feel in
the least like . . . me!"

"It is a transformation!"

"*Monsieur* Worth has been very kind. He did not
wish to see me at first, as he is tired and intends leaving
the country in a few days."

"How did you persuade him?" the Duke enquired,
still so bemused by Antonia's appearance that he found
it hard to collect his thoughts.

She laughed.

"I was ready to go down on my knees in front of
him, but when he saw me he was so horrified at my
appearance that I think he considered it a challenge!"

Antonia sighed contentedly.

"I am so glad you are pleased."

"I suppose I am," the Duke replied. "At the same
time, I can see that from now on my role of husband is
going to be rather different from what I had envisaged!"

He did not have to explain to Antonia what he meant,
for she exclaimed delightedly:

"That is a compliment and the first you have paid
me!"

"Have I really been so remiss?" the Duke enquired.

"You have had nothing to compliment me about,"
she said, "and do not bother to tell me how terrible I
looked! *Monsieur* Worth has said it both in French and
in English!"

She gave a little laugh before she went on:

"What is so exciting is that he is coming to England in a month's time and he has already begun to plan a winter trousseau for me. I only hope you are as rich as you are reputed to be!"

"I can see that sooner or later it is going to be a choice between clothes and horses!" the Duke said.

"That is unkind!" Antonia flashed at him. "You know quite well which I should choose!"

It was strange, the Duke thought, as the day progressed, that instead of sitting and talking seriously to Antonia as he had done previously, he now found it quite easy to flirt with his own wife!

It was absurd that clothes should make so much difference, but he knew that instead of being an unfledged country-girl with whom he had nothing in common but horses, she had now in her Worth gown assumed an aura of glamour.

And yet her eyes were still very innocent and he found himself watching them reflecting her reaction to everything that happened and to everything he said to her.

After luncheon they called on some friends the Duke had known on his last visit and inevitably the conversation was of war.

"I do not mind telling you, Duke," one of the guests said pompously, "that I have taken a very large wager that war will be declared, if not tonight, tomorrow!"

"Are you not worried?" Antonia asked.

The Frenchman who had spoken smiled.

"Here in Paris we are as safe as—how do you say, in your country?—the Bank of England!" he answered. "And it will only be a few days before our magnificent Army puts those Prussians, once and for all, in their proper place!"

"I have heard that their troops are well trained," the Duke said, "and the railways in Germany in recent years have been planned with a particular eye to Military needs."

"We have something far more important," the Frenchman replied. "We have a destructive device in the cartridge-firing *chassepot* rifle which has nearly twice the range of the Dreyse 'needle-gun.' And we also have a secret weapon called the *mitrailleuse*."

"What is that?" someone asked.

"It is a gun consisting of a bundle of twenty-five barrels which by turning a handle can be fired off in very rapid succession."

The speaker gave a loud laugh.

"The Germans have no answer to that!"

The Duke said nothing, but he was thinking that he had heard of a steel breech-loading cannon which *Herr* Krupp had made for Prussia but which at the time the French Military leaders had refused to take seriously.

When they drove back to their house from the Reception Antonia asked:

"You do not think there will be a war?"

"I hope not," the Duke replied. "But if there is it will not be fought here, but in Germany."

"Do you think the French can advance without the Germans stopping them?"

"That is what they believe," the Duke replied.

He had already told Antonia they were dining that night with the Marquise de Barouche before a Ball that she was giving in her magnificent Château near the Bois.

As she changed for dinner Antonia was not only thrilled with the wonderful gown that Worth had delivered for her to wear, but also the fact that she had a French maid.

It was one more arrangement which had been made by the Courier who had gone ahead of them. He had engaged a French woman so that Antonia would be properly looked after when she arrived in Paris.

It was typical, she thought, that everything that concerned the Duke was meticulously planned down to the very smallest detail.

She knew that when she returned to England, Mr. Graham would have engaged an English maid to look after her and one who was experienced in attending to riding-habits.

The French maid was vivacious and very efficient.

She chatted away gaily as she arranged Antonia's hair in the manner the *Coiffeur* had done who had come to *Monsieur* Worth's while he was fitting Antonia into the gown in which she had dazzled the Duke at luncheon.

"For no other lady, however important or grand she might be, Your Grace, would I put myself to such trouble," *Monsieur* Worth had said.

"Then why am I so honoured, *Monsieur?*" Antonia had enquired.

"Because, Your Grace, I am English, like yourself, and I am fed up with the French always expecting an Englishwoman to look dowdy, ungainly, and to have protruding teeth, as most of them do!"

They had both laughed but Antonia knew it was not only patriotism which made the great man take so much trouble. She also, as she had told the Duke, presented a challenge he could not resist.

"Why did I never realise," she asked herself as she looked in the mirror, "that I had such a good figure?"

She knew the answer was that her mother would have been outraged by the thought of her being conceited about anything so immodest.

Her long neck, her ears which were perfectly shell-shaped, her huge eyes, now that they were fully revealed by the up-swept darkness of her hair, were all new and exciting discoveries.

When she went into the Salon where the Duke was waiting to take her out to dinner, wearing a gown of golden-orange tulle, glittering with diamanté and ornamented with mimosa, she felt for the first time in her life glamourous and romantic.

She saw the glint of admiration in the Duke's eyes as he looked at her, and as she walked towards him she felt she was on a stage waiting for the plaudits of the audience.

"Do you approve?" she asked, as he did not speak.

Now there was a touch of anxiety in her eyes.

"I am very proud to be your escort!" he answered,

and saw the colour come into her cheeks because she
was so delighted by his reply.

If she had any doubts left, they were soon dispelled
by the compliments that were paid to her by the dinner-
party guests and the flirtatious attitude of both her partners at dinner.

"You are enchanting—fascinating!"

"I would never have believed that a star could fall
from the sky so early in the evening!"

Antonia told herself that she might have found such
exaggeration incredible, but despite her inexperience of
men she could not help realising that their admiration
was sincere.

In fact as soon as the Ball opened she was besieged
with partners in a way which made her realise that this
was an experience very different from anything that
had ever happened to her before.

She returned to the Duke's side after waltzing with a
handsome and ardent young Diplomat.

"You are enjoying yourself?" he asked.

"It is wonderful! More wonderful than I could ever
have imagined!" Antonia replied. "But I would
like . . ."

She was about to say that she would like to dance
with him, when their conversation was interrupted by a
cry of joy.

"Athol! *Mon Brave!* Why did no-one tell me you
were in Paris?"

An entrancingly pretty woman was holding out both
hands to the Duke and looking up into his face in a
manner which proclaimed all too obviously her interest
in him.

"Ludevica!" the Duke exclaimed. "I heard that you
had returned to Vienna."

"We went—we came back!" the lady answered. "I
missed you—*Hálas!* How I missed you!"

She spoke in a fascinating manner which seemed to
make every word have a hidden meaning, both intimate
and provocative.

She was holding both the Duke's hands in hers and as if he suddenly remembered Antonia's existence, he said:

"I am here on my honeymoon and we have only just arrived. May I present my wife—*Madame La Comtesse* de Rezonville."

The nod that Antonia received was so brief as to be almost insulting. Then the Comtesse was holding on to the Duke's arm and looking up into his eyes.

She made it obvious that whatever they had meant to each other in the past, her feelings at any rate were unchanged.

Because she felt embarrassed and at a loss how to behave in such circumstances, Antonia glanced round the Ball-Room and almost immediately her next partner was at her side.

She allowed herself to be escorted onto the dancefloor only to look back and see the Duke with the Comtesse hanging on to his arm, disappearing through one of the open windows which led into the garden.

There were Chinese lanterns hanging from the branches of the trees, but otherwise the shadows were dark.

As Antonia had already discovered, there were small arbours discreetly arranged where there were soft cushioned seats and the reassurance that anything that was said could not be overheard.

She could not help feeling that even if the Duke had not asked her to dance he might have taken her into the garden.

If the Marchioness had been present, that was where, she was quite certain, they would have ended up.

She gave a little sigh, then thought to herself that if the Duke had been thinking of the Marchioness while they were on their way to Paris and perhaps earlier today, he would certainly not be thinking of her now!

Never had Antonia seen anyone quite so fascinating as the Comtesse de Rezonville.

She gathered from the reference to Vienna that she was in fact Viennese. Her hair was certainly the deep,

dark red beloved of the Austrian women who all
wished to look like their beautiful Empress.

Yet her eyes were dark, almost purple in their depths,
while at the same time they sparkled as everything
about her had seemed to glitter and shimmer.

She had made Antonia feel that however elegantly
she might be dressed in a Worth creation, there was
something lacking inside herself which the Comtesse
had in super-abundance.

"You are very pensive," her partner said, breaking
in her thoughts.

"I was thinking," Antonia replied.

"I wish it could be of me!"

"But I do not know you!"

"That is something that can easily be rectified," he
replied. "When may I see you again? Where are you
staying in Paris?"

She laughed at him because they were questions that
had been asked by all her partners.

The dance came to an end and another Frenchman
drew her onto the dance-floor.

Although Antonia glanced frequently towards the
windows, there was no sign of the Duke returning, nor
could she see the fascinating Comtesse.

She lost count of her partners. Then she found herself dancing with a man to whom she did not remember
being introduced. She was quite certain he had not
written his name on her dance-card.

It did not seem to matter if she exchanged one man
for another. They all seemed to say much the same
thing, and she was really hoping the Duke would appear so that they could go home.

"You are the Duchess of Doncaster?" her new partner asked as he swung her round to the music of the
"Blue Danube."

He spoke in a heavy voice, almost as if it were an
indictment.

"Yes, I am," Antonia replied. "But I have a feeling
we have not been introduced."

"Your husband is with you?"

"Yes, of course," Antonia answered. "We are on our honeymoon."

Her partner glanced round the room.

"I do not see him anywhere."

"He is in the garden," Antonia replied, "with a very fascinating and alluring lady whom I suspect of being an old friend and who was certainly very pleased to see him."

"What was her name?"

The question was so sharp, so abrupt, that Antonia looked at the man in surprise and almost missed a step.

"The Comtesse de Rezonville."

"So! It is what I suspected!" the Frenchman muttered in a furious tone.

He stopped dancing and, taking Antonia by the arm, drew her across the room towards the open window.

"We will find them," he said grimly, "doubtless, as you say, in the garden."

There was something so ferocious in the way he spoke that Antonia said quickly:

"I . . . I may have been . . . mistaken. Who . . . who are you? And why are you so interested in my husband?"

"I happen to be married to the fascinating, alluring lady you have just described so vividly!" he replied.

Antonia's heart gave a frightened leap.

She realised by the way he spoke and the manner in which he was pulling her along that the Comte was in a rage and she knew she had precipitated it by what she had told him.

"How could I have known," she asked herself frantically, "that the man dancing with me was the Comtesse's husband?"

They walked down the steps which led from the terrace into the garden.

The Comte stood looking round as if he was adjusting his eyes from the brilliant lights of the Ball-Room to the darkness which was relieved only by the golden glow of the Chinese lanterns.

"I am sure they are not here," Antonia said hastily. "Let us look in the Supper-Room."

The Comte did not answer her but kept his hand firmly on her arm, pulling her forward and moving her towards the right.

Bordering the lawn there was the first of the arbours screened by ferns or potted-plants where they were not naturally enveloped with climbing roses or flowering creepers.

Still dragging Antonia with him, he went up to the first arbour, disturbing a couple who were kissing each other passionately, and who looked round with a startled expression on their faces.

"Pardon, Monsieur, pardon, Madame," the Comte muttered, and moved towards the next arbour.

Antonia stood still.

"Stop!" she said. "You cannot do this! I do not know what you suspect, but whatever it is, it is quite unfounded. My husband and I are here on our honeymoon. We have only just arrived. I think he will be looking for me in the Ball-Room."

"You will find your husband, *Madame,* when we find my wife!" the Comte replied.

He drew Antonia on again and she knew that unless she made a scene she could do nothing but go with him.

He was very strong and his fingers seemed to dig into the softness of her arm.

There was a grim determination about him which she found terrifying and which made her feel at the same time weak and helpless.

They visited no less than four arbours and interrupted the couples in them in an embarrassing manner which made Antonia hope that while she could see their faces in the light from the lanterns hanging on the trees, they could not see hers.

Then just as they approached the fifth arbour she heard the Duke's voice.

She could not hear what he said but there was no mistaking his deep resonant tone.

Because she was afraid that he might be embracing the Comtesse or indulging in any of the small intimacies they had seen when interrupting the other couples, she called out:

"Athol! Athol! Where are you?"

She knew her cry annoyed the Comte and he looked at her angrily.

Then he moved her forward quickly, still clasping her arm. In the arbour the Duke and the Comtesse were sitting beside each other on the cushioned seat.

There was nothing to show they had been doing anything intimate, but even if they had, Antonia thought with satisfaction, they would have had time to move apart when she had called out to the Duke.

When they saw the Comte it seemed to Antonia as if, for a moment, both the Duke and the Comtesse were carved in stone.

Then the Comtesse gave a little cry.

"Jacques, what an enchanting surprise!" she exclaimed. "I was not expecting you to join me."

"That is obvious!" the Comte replied, and his eyes were on the Duke.

"Good evening, Rezonville," the Duke said calmly. "I have only just learnt that you have returned to Paris."

"I warned you when you were here last to keep away from my wife!" the Comte said aggressively.

"My dear fellow," the Duke said, "your wife was just congratulating me, as I hope you will, on my marriage."

"My congratulations are best expressed like this!" the Comte replied.

He was wearing only one glove and he held the other in his right hand.

Now he raised it and slapped the Duke across the face.

The Comtesse gave a shrill cry while Antonia felt as if the breath had been squeezed out of her body.

"I consider that an insult!" the Duke said quietly.

"That is what it is meant to be!" the Comte retorted. "My seconds will wait on you!"

"I have no intention of waiting," the Comte replied. "We will fight at dawn."

"Certainly!" the Duke replied.

He moved past the Comte and offered his arm to Antonia.

"I think it is time we said farewell to our hostess," he said in a quiet, level voice that was quite expressionless.

Antonia was glad to put her hand on his arm. She had the feeling that otherwise she might have fallen to the ground.

They moved back through the garden towards the house, and as they did so they could hear the Comtesse screaming at her husband, and the anger in his voice as he answered her.

It was impossible to speak—impossible to say anything until the Duke led Antonia into the lighted Ball-Room where the Marquise was standing at the door saying farewell to others of her guests.

"It has been a delightful evening," the Duke said graciously.

"I am so glad you could both come," the Marquise answered. "If you are to be in Paris for some time we must meet again."

"My wife and I will be delighted!" the Duke replied.

He kissed the Marquise's hand, Antonia curtseyed gracefully, and soon they were driving away towards the Champs Élysées in the carriage that had been waiting for them.

"What does it . . . mean? You cannot . . . fight him!" Antonia said frantically, as the Duke did not speak.

"I have no alternative," he replied. "I must apologise, Antonia, for what must have been a very upsetting experience for you, but the Comte has wanted an excuse to call me out for some time."

Remembering the way the Comtesse had greeted the Duke, Antonia thought that perhaps he had every reason for jealousy, but all she could say in a frightened voice was:

"He may . . . kill you!"

"That is unlikely," the Duke replied. "Most duels are fairly civilised. A small show of blood, and honour is satisfied!"

"Can you be . . . sure of that?" Antonia asked.

She was thinking of the Comte's anger and the aggressive manner in which he had deliberately insulted the Duke.

"I assure you, Antonia," the Duke said, "there is nothing to trouble you. By the time you wake tomorrow morning it will all be over!"

"M-may I . . . go with you?" Antonia asked.

"No, of course you may not!" the Duke replied. "Spectators are not permitted on such occasions! I assure you the whole thing is just a formality—a salve to the Comte's pride."

"The Comtesse is very attractive," Antonia said.

"Very!" the Duke answered. "And I assure you I am not the first man to have found her so!"

"Then why are you fighting over her?"

"It is a question of honour," the Duke replied. "I am quite prepared to admit, since we are frank with each other, Antonia, that the Comte might have reason to be incensed with me."

"But you . . . cannot fight . . . every man who is . . . jealous of you!" Antonia said hesitatingly.

"I hope not!" the Duke smiled. "But Rezonville has always been a fiery, over-dramatic fellow. At one time he talked of challenging the Emperor to a duel, but fortunately he was persuaded not to make a fool of himself."

"Could not . . . someone persuade him . . . now?" Antonia asked in a very small voice.

"I am not an Emperor!" the Duke answered. "And I assure you I am not afraid of Rezonville or any other man!"

It seemed there was nothing more to be said. When they reached the house the Duke, having escorted Antonia into the hall, raised her hand to his lips.

"You will understand that I have arrangements to

make," he said. "Sleep well, Antonia. I hope when we have breakfast tomorrow morning all this unpleasantness will be forgotten."

She wanted to hold on to him.

She had a feeling she ought not to let him go, but he turned and went out of the house and she heard the carriage drive away.

She stood indecisively in the Hall and the night-footman who had let them in waited as if he expected her to give him an order.

Antonia made up her mind.

"Fetch Tour to me immediately!" she said.

"Très bien, Madame."

The footman hurried up the stairs to fetch the Duke's valet and Antonia went into the Salon.

*   *   *

It was still very dark under the trees although there was a faint glow in the East while the stars were fading overhead.

Tour led the way through the bushes and shrubs and Antonia followed closely behind him, frightened of losing him in the shadows.

After the Duke had left the house, it had taken a great deal of persuasion to make Tour promise he would take her to the Bois. It was only when she threatened to go alone that he finally consented.

"I don't know what His Grace will say to me," he kept murmuring unhappily.

"I will take the blame, Tour. You know as well as I do that you cannot disobey my orders. I command you to take me to the Bois where we can watch the duel just in case His Grace is hurt and needs assistance."

The valet still looked unhappy and Antonia said:

"If His Grace is unharmed, then we will slip away and be back at the house long before he returns."

She had known that it would be difficult to do what she wished and she had actually heaved a sigh of relief when Tour had finally consented.

He had been with the Duke for years and always travelled with him when he went abroad.

In England the Duke had two younger valets also in attendance, but Tour spoke several foreign languages.

Because she wanted to find out more about the Comte, Antonia insisted on Tour sitting inside the carriage as they drove to the Bois.

She knew he was embarrassed that she should request anything so unusual, and he sat opposite her on the small seat, his back straight, his hat held firmly in both his hands.

"Tell me about the Comte de Rezonville," Antonia asked. "Is he a good shot?"

"He has a reputation, Your Grace, for having fought a number of duels."

"All over the Comtesse?" Antonia asked, and felt it was a foolish question with only one answer. "Has he ever threatened the Duke before?"

"There was a little trouble two years ago, Your Grace."

"What sort of trouble?"

Tour looked uncomfortable.

"I can guess," Antonia said hastily, "but the Comte did not challenge the Duke on that occasion?"

"He threatened to, but as His Grace was staying in the British Embassy with the Ambassador, I think *Monsieur le Comte* thought it might cause an international incident."

"I see!" Antonia answered.

The Duke now was without the protection of the British Flag and therefore the Comte could take the vengeance which must have been festering in him for two years.

She was suddenly desperately afraid.

As if he knew what she was feeling, Tour said:

"Don't you take on, Your Grace. It'll be all right. There's no-one handles a pistol better than His Grace, and he's a sportsman if ever there was one!"

"I am sure he is going to be all right!" Antonia said, speaking more to herself than to Tour.

At the same time, there was a fear within her which seemed almost like a presentiment of evil.

She could see the clearing in the wood as she peeped through the bushes into which Tour had taken her.

She realised it was the traditional place where the famous Parisian duels were fought and wondered how many men had died in just this spot simply because they had aroused jealousy and anger over some tiresome woman.

There was, however, little time for introspection.

The duellists were already lined up. She could see the Duke conferring with his seconds and the Comte conferring with his.

There was a man who she imagined was the Referee and another holding a black bag, who she guessed with a sinking of her heart was a Doctor.

Dawn had broken and now it was easy to see every detail, the diamond tie-pin glittering in the Comte's cravat, the Duke's signet ring on his little finger.

"I cannot bear it!" Antonia thought.

She wondered if she should run forward and beg them not to fight each other, but she knew she would only embarrass the Duke and that she would be sent away.

If the duel did not take place this morning, it would take place tomorrow.

She fastened her teeth onto her lower lip so that she would not cry out.

Now the Referee was ready and he called the two contestants to him and they stood back to back.

"Ten paces," Antonia heard him say and began to count.

"*Un, deux, trois . . .*"

The Duke was taller than the Comte and he moved slowly and with a dignity which made Antonia feel very proud.

There was something magnificent about him, she thought. Something which seemed to raise him above everything that was squalid and vulgar and made him a man of honour and a sportsman in every fibre of his being.

"*Huit, neuf, dix!*"

Antonia held her breath.

The Duke and the Comte stood sideways to each other and brought their pistols, French fashion, down upon their left arms, which were raised shoulder high, and took aim.

"Fire!"

The Referee gave the word and the Duke with superb marksmanship just grazed the outside of the Comte's arm. A crimson patch appeared on his coat.

The Duke's seconds moved forward.

"Honour is satisfied!" they declared.

The Duke dropped his arms.

"Not as far as I am concerned!" the Comte replied savagely.

Then he fired!

There was the reverberation of his pistol, and Antonia realised that when the Duke had lowered both his arms, he had been off guard and at his ease. He had also turned his body fully towards the Comte.

Just for a moment she thought the bullet had missed, then as the Duke fell she gave a cry that was strangled in her throat and ran towards him.

She was certain as she reached him that he was dead!

Chapter Five

Someone . . . a man . . . was screaming . . . crying
out . . . making a noise. . . .

The Duke wondered how anyone could be so tiresome when he felt so ill. He had heard this man before
and resented the commotion which he made.

He could still hear him but he was further away . . .
in the distance . . . gradually fading . . . until there was
silence. . . .

He felt a relief that the noise was no longer there,
and then a soft voice which he also seemed to have
heard many times said:

"Go to sleep. You are safe . . . quite safe. No one
shall hurt you."

He wanted to say that he was not afraid, but it was
too much effort to try to speak or to open his eyes.

"Go to sleep, my darling," the voice said tenderly.
"But perhaps you are thirsty?"

There was an arm lifting his head very carefully so
that he could drink from a glass which contained something cool and rather sweet.

He was not certain what it was—it was too much of
an effort to try to think.

It was strangely comforting to be held closely and his
cheek was against something very soft.

There was a sweet fragrance of flowers and now there
was a cool hand on his forehead, soothing him, mes-
merising him, and he knew he was slipping away into
oblivion. . . .

The Duke came back to consciousness to hear two voices speaking.

"How is he, Tour?"

It was the voice of a woman and vaguely he wondered who she was. Tour he recognised as his valet.

"Much quieter, Your Grace. I have washed His Grace, shaved him, and he hardly moved."

"Did the Doctor come while I was asleep?"

"He did, Your Grace, and he is very pleased indeed with the wound. He said His Grace must have been in the pink of condition to be healing so quickly."

"You should have awakened me, Tour, I would have liked to talk to the Doctor."

"You must sleep sometimes, Your Grace. You cannot be up all night and all day."

"I am all right. There are many more important things to worry about rather than my health."

"You have to think of yourself, Your Grace. Remember, I cannot cope without you, especially when His Grace is in one of his restless moods."

"No, that is true. Will you sit with him a little longer, Tour? I am expecting Mr. Labouchere."

"Yes, of course, Your Grace, and afterwards I think you should take a little fresh air."

"I will go into the garden. You will call me if His Grace wakes or is restless?"

"I will do that, Your Grace. I have given my promise and I won't break it."

"Thank you, Tour."

The Duke wondered what it was all about but he was too tired to make the effort of trying to find out. He fell asleep.

* * *

Antonia waited in the Salon for Henry Labouchere.

She was sure that when the Duke regained consciousness he would think it strange that the only friend she had in Paris was a journalist.

Henry Labouchere, as it happened, owned a quarter

share in the *London Daily News,* and had appointed himself to the Paris office.

An Englishman with Huguenot ancestry, "Labby," as all his friends called him, was a character. While many people hated him for his sharp and caustic articles, he was many other things as well.

A wit, cynic, stage manager, and diplomat, he had filled all these roles and had been elected to Parliament as a Radical and a Republican in 1865.

He had, however, lost his seat at the same time as he had inherited 250,000 pounds, and he now devoted himself to increasing the circulation of the *Daily News.*

Henry Labouchere had come to interview the Duke, having heard rumours of the duel which had taken place in the Bois.

He had found instead a white-faced and very frightened Duchess who told him quite frankly that the Duke's life was in danger and pleaded with him not to write about it in his newspaper.

Henry Labouchere, who had been the lover of a great many attractive women, found Antonia's pleading, worried eyes irresistible.

He not only promised to keep the duel a secret, but as the days passed he became her friend, confidant, and adviser when she had no one else to turn to.

It was Henry Labouchere who kept her up to date with the fantastic events which were happening in Paris.

At first, when everyone expected the war to be over almost immediately, the French went on enjoying themselves without a thought that there might be anything to disturb their pleasure but a celebration of French victories.

On July 28, the Emperor had taken command of his Armies, with the Empress's words, "Louis, do your duty well," ringing in his ears.

But as he passed through Metz he was in constant pain from the stone in his bladder and to many of his Generals he gave the impression of a man who was utterly worn out.

The Germans had 400,000 men in supreme fighting

trim and 1,440 guns concentrated on the far side of the Rhine, while Louis Napoleon had been able to muster only 250,000 soldiers.

His strategic plan was to advance rapidly eastwards into Germany in the hope of swinging the South German States and eventually the reluctant Austrians into war against Prussia.

The gay uniforms of the French Army, the joyous fanfares, the confident and dashing Officers with their smart "imperials" worn as a compliment to their Emperor, all made a striking contrast to the Prussian disdain for any kind of ostentation.

On August 2, the French captured Saarbrüchen from the weak German advance forces and all Paris revelled in the triumph.

A telegram was read out on the Bourse reporting the capture of the Prussian Crown Prince. This caused a famous tenor to sing the "Marseillaise" from the top of a horse-drawn bus!

Henry Labouchere had related to Antonia the wild scenes that took place in the streets.

She had heard and seen nothing as she nursed a delirious and restless Duke, who was running a high fever after the bullet had been extracted from his wound.

At first she was not particularly interested in the news, and although she thanked Mr. Labouchere for coming to see her, she made it obvious that she could spend only a few minutes with him.

All her thoughts were concentrated on the sick-bed.

However, as the week went by and the Duke, though his wound was improving day by day, did not regain consciousness, she found it was impossible to shut her mind to the events occurring outside.

She therefore found herself looking forward to Mr. Labouchere's visits even though he brought her little but bad news.

Stories of terrible inefficiency drifted back to Paris; of weary troops reaching their destination to find their tents had been mislaid; of gunmen separated from their guns; of magazines discovered to be empty.

After two defeats at Spicheren and Woerth, a long and disheartening retreat began. Orders and counter-orders were issued from a panic-stricken Paris.

A German attack at St. Privat on August 18 inflicted twenty thousand casualties on the French and during the night the Army fled back in disorder to Metz, from where they had started.

The disastrous news had staggered Paris into a state which was, as Mr. Labouchere put it, "bordering upon madness."

"I have just seen three or four Germans nearly punched to death," he told Antonia. "Several of the larger cafés have been forced to close! Excited mobs are attacking them because their proprietors are supposed to have German sympathies."

What seemed to Antonia to distress him even more was when he told her that the beautiful trees in the Bois were being felled.

"Is everyone leaving Paris?" she asked a few days later.

"On the contrary," he replied. "The French authorities are insisting that it is safer to be in Paris than anywhere else, and people are flooding into the City."

"Then things cannot be too bad." Antonia smiled.

"I do hope you are right," he said. "At the same time, I would have liked you and your husband to go home while it is possible."

"It is quite impossible at the moment," Antonia replied, "and surely we are completely safe being British?"

"I expect so," he answered. "But I do advise you against going outside the house except into your own garden. People are arrested on the most trivial suspicions of being a German, and there has been a certain amount of dissention on the Boulevards."

"In what way?" Antonia asked.

"When the despatches arrive and they are not favourable, the crowds start shouting: 'Down with the Emperor!' and *'Déchéance!'* "

"Abdication!" Antonia exclaimed. "Can they really be asking that?"

"The French are very intolerant of failure," Henry Labouchere replied.

Because she felt that it might be a long time before they could return to England and therefore they must not be extravagant with what money they had, Antonia, after consultation with Tour, dismissed the majority of the servants in the house.

She kept two who had been there with its owners, a middle-aged couple who were quite content to do everything that was required, as there was no entertaining.

Antonia found that Tour was a tower of strength. Not only could he speak French fluently, but he knew exactly how to handle the Duke and was, in his own way, she thought, an even better Nurse than she was.

It was Tour who told her of the animals massed in the Bois and for the first time Antonia faced the suggestion that the Germans might reach Paris.

"So much food will not be necessary?" she asked Tour in surprise.

"One never knows, Your Grace," he replied in a tone which told her he did not wish to make her nervous. "They say it would be impossible for anyone to take Paris, it is so heavily fortified."

"That is true," Antonia agreed. "I was reading in the Guide Book how the whole City is surrounded by an *enceinte* wall, thirty-foot high and divided into ninety-three bastions. Besides, there is a moat and at varying distances a chain of powerful forts."

She thought of the animals again and said:

"But of course all the trains will be needed to convey food to the troops at the Front, and I quite understand that in the City we should be self-sufficient."

She asked Henry Labouchere for further news when he next came to see her, and in reply he handed her an article he had written for the *Daily News* in England.

She read it, her eyes widening with surprise at the incredible story.

As far as the eye can reach over every open space, down the long, long Avenue all the way to Longchamps itself, there is nothing but sheep, sheep, sheep! In the Bois alone there must be 250,000, as well as 40,000 oxen.

*   *   *

"Can this really be true?" she enquired.

"We are getting ourselves prepared," Henry Labouchere had laughed, "so you need not be afraid that when the Duke gets better he will not be able to build up his strength with plenty of good meat."

Tour, however, was not prepared to rely entirely on the Bois. He brought into the house quite a lot of food which would not deteriorate, telling Antonia gloomily that it was getting more expensive every day.

The Duke stirred and instantly Antonia rose from a chair at the open window and came to the side of the bed.

She knelt down beside him and said in the soft voice which he had grown used to hearing these past weeks:

"Are you hot? Would you like a drink, my darling?"

She spoke, he thought, as a woman would speak to a child she loved.

He remembered that when he had been delirious he had thought that his mother had her arms around him and that she was telling him to be good and go to sleep.

He felt very weak and yet for the first time his brain was clear. He knew who he was and remembered that he was in Paris.

Then, as he tried to move, he felt a sudden pain in his chest. He recalled the duel and that it would account for what he now knew had been a long illness.

Antonia had lifted him very gently; now she was feeding him with a soup that he thought must be extremely nourishing as it tasted of beef, or was it perhaps venison? He could not be certain.

She placed it against his lips, giving him small spoonfuls, waiting between each one so that he had time to swallow.

There was again the fragrance of flowers coming from her, and when he had taken quite a considerable amount of the soup, she held him close for a moment.

He found that the softness he had felt beneath his cheek so many times before had been the softness of her breast.

"You are better," she said, and there was a note of elation in her voice. "The Doctor will be very pleased with you tomorrow, and now, my dearest one, you must go back to sleep again."

He felt her hand cool against his forehead.

"No fever," she said as if she spoke to herself. "How wonderful it will be when it is all gone and you are yourself."

She laid him down against the pillows, moving them comfortably behind his head. Then she moved away and after a little while he opened his eyes.

He had not realised before that it was night-time. There was a candle lit beside his bed, the curtains were drawn back, and the windows were open. He thought he could see the sky and the stars.

He lay trying to focus his eyes, and then, as if she knew instinctively that he was awake, Antonia came back to the bed.

She looked down at him and said in a voice that was a little above a whisper:

"Athol, can you hear me?"

He found it impossible to speak but he turned his eyes to look at her.

She made a little sound that was a cry of delight.

"You are awake!" she exclaimed. "And I think you can understand."

She knelt down beside him, taking his hand in hers, and said softly:

"Everything is all right. You are going to get well and there is nothing to make you afraid."

*   *   *

Henry Labouchere, looking rather raffish, Antonia thought, came to call at four o'clock in the afternoon.

Tour had let him in and Antonia came into the Salon wearing one of her elegant Worth gowns which revealed her exquisite figure.

"You look happy," he said, and raised her hand to his lips.

"I am," she replied. "My invalid has eaten a proper meal today for the first time. He is sitting up in bed and being rather irritable, which Tour tells me is a good sign."

Labby laughed.

"Well, that is a relief at any rate! Perhaps now you will be able to give me more attention."

Antonia looked at him in surprise as he went on:

"I do not think I have ever spent so much time with a woman who would not even know I existed, had the news I brought her not in some way concerned her husband."

Labby spoke respectfully and Antonia laughed. Then she said seriously:

"You know how grateful I am. I should have known nothing of what is happening and been very much more afraid if you had not proved such a very kind friend."

"Friend!" Labby ejaculated. "That is not what I wish to be, as you must be well aware! This friendship, as you call it, will ruin my reputation as a lady-killer!"

"It is a . . . friendship I value very much," Antonia said softly.

She was used by this time to Labby's protestations of love to her, even while he realised better than she did how hopeless it was.

He had never met a woman who concentrated so fiercely on a man who could neither see nor hear her and who from all accounts was not particularly interested anyway.

Labby knew of the Duke's liaison with the Marchioness and his reputation with beautiful women. He did not need Antonia to tell him—which she would not have thought of doing—why the Duke had married.

Labby had at first been touched by Antonia's youth and inexperience.

Then as he saw her day after day, calling at first because he told himself she was a country-woman whom he must help and if possible protect, he found himself falling in love.

He could hardly believe it possible that at the age of thirty-nine he should find himself as idealistically enamoured as he had been when in his youth he had once joined a Mexican Circus in pursuit of a lady acrobat.

Yet there was something about Antonia which told him she was different from any of the women he had pursued so ardently in his varied career.

At one time Queen Victoria had referred to him as "that viper, Labouchere!" She would have been surprised how controlled, gentle, and considerate he was to Antonia.

Labby did not only bring Antonia the news, he also made her laugh, something she had almost forgotten to do in her anxiety over the Duke.

Because the eyes of the world were focussed on France, inquisitive British and Americans were flooding into the City. Labby had related that enterprising Estate Agents were circulating advertisements which read:

Notice for the benefit of English gentlemen wishing to attend the Siege of Paris: comfortable apartments, completely shell-proof, rooms in the basement for impressionable personages.

"The Siege of Paris!" Antonia had repeated apprehensively. "Can it possibly come to that?"

"No, of course not," Labby had said confidently. "The Germans will be driven back long before they reach Paris. But there is no doubt that the Army is somewhat disorganised and has retired to the small citadel town of Sedan."

He paused before he added:

"Things cannot be too bad. I hear the French Cavalry blades gave a Ball at Douzy last night. It was attended by all the ladies from Sedan who are to watch a triumphant victory tomorrow."

There was no triumph! Two days later, Labby had to tell Antonia that the Army was trapped with two powerful Prussian Armies moving in.

There was only enough food in Sedan for a few days.

What Labby did not relate to Antonia, even if he was aware of it, was that there was chaos inside Sedan reaching catastrophic proportions. Cannons were jammed wheel wheel with refugee wagons, while shells from four hundred Prussian guns burst in their midst.

Then on September 1 came the bomb-shell. After Louis Napoleon had ridden amongst his wavering troops outside the walls of Sedan, his face rouged in order to hide how ill he was, he finally had to order a white flag to be hoisted over the citadel.

It was two days later before the contradictory rumours, and there were many of them, reached Paris.

Labby told Antonia that the Empress had flown into a terrible Spanish rage and then retired to her room to weep.

In the streets now there was no doubt of the menacing roar of the crowd or the cry that was heard everywhere:

"*Déchéance! Dé-ché-ance! Dé-ché-ance!*"

*   *   *

"What is the news today?" Antonia asked nervously on September 4.

It was difficult, because she was so pleased about the improvement in the Duke's health, to force herself to attend to the troubles which were happening outside the house.

She felt sometimes as if they were alone on an island, surrounded by a hostile sea and yet somehow protected from it.

"Paris has learnt that the Emperor has offered up his sword," Labby replied. "And the Empress at last has consented to leave."

Antonia started. She had felt that as long as the Empress stayed in Paris, things could not be too bad.

"Her Majesty stayed on at the Tuileries until the servants began to desert her, flinging off their livery and pilfering as they went. It was nearly too late," Labby told Antonia. "The mob was accumulating outside and she must have heard the clatter of their muskets in the court-yard and their voices on the main staircase."

"Did she get away?" Antonia asked quickly.

"She left by a side door accompanied by her lady-in-waiting. She was heavily veiled and I have learnt that the two ladies went first to the house of the State Chancellor in the Boulevard Haussman, but he had already gone. Eventually, after finding the same thing at the house of her Chamberlain, Her Majesty found shelter with her American Dentist, a Dr. Evans."

"How extraordinary!" Antonia exclaimed.

"It was sensible, if slightly unconventional," Labby remarked.

The following day Labby was taken by Antonia into the Duke's bed-room. She had already related to him how kind the English journalist had been during the long, frightening weeks of his unconsciousness.

She thought the Duke was slightly sceptical—or was it suspicious?—of the warm manner in which she had described Henry Labouchere.

But when she brought him into the bed-room he had held out his hand and said in his most pleasant tone:

"I hear, Labouchere, I have to be very grateful to you."

"There is no reason for you to be grateful, Your Grace," Henry Labouchere replied. "It has been a very great pleasure to be of service to the Duchess."

He smiled at Antonia as he spoke and there was an expression on his raffish face which made the Duke look at him sharply.

What he had suspected was confirmed during the conversation which followed.

Even a less-experienced man than the Duke would have noticed the gentleness in Henry Labouchere's voice when he addressed Antonia, and the manner in which he found it hard to take his eyes from her.

"We must leave Paris as soon as I am well enough to travel," the Duke remarked abruptly.

"I am afraid that will not be for some time," Labby replied. "As Your Grace must know by now, you have been very ill indeed."

He smiled at Antonia again as he added:

"I shall be giving away no secrets if I tell you, now the danger is over, that your Doctor told me it was a ninety-per-cent certainty that you would die."

Antonia drew in her breath.

"I . . . did . . . not realise it was as bad . . . as that," she faltered.

"You were saved by two things," Labby told the Duke. "The first, that the bullet missed your heart and by a miracle did not shatter any bones, and secondly that you were outstandingly fit."

"I am glad you did not tell me until now," Antonia said.

"Do you imagine that I would have distressed you more than you were already?" he asked gently.

The Duke listened to this exchange, looking first at Henry Labouchere, then at Antonia.

"I would be grateful, Labouchere," he said after a moment, "if you would tell me exactly what the position is at the moment. As you can imagine, I have a great deal to catch up with and women are never very good at describing the horrors of war."

"Her Grace will have told you that there is a new Government," Henry Labouchere replied. "The Second Empire has ended ignominiously and France has been humiliated. King William has reached Rheims."

"It is hard to believe!" the Duke exclaimed.

"But France still has an Army of sorts, all of which

General Trochu, our new leader, is concentrating in Paris."

"Is that wise?" the Duke enquired.

"He has little choice," Labby conceded, "and the enrolment of three hundred fifty thousand able-bodied males in the National Guard is encouraging, while at the same time it reveals the inefficiency of France's war mobilization."

"I should think that the fortifications will certainly make Paris impregnable," the Duke remarked.

"A visit to the fortifications is rapidly replacing a drive in the Bois as the smart Parisian Sunday-afternoon entertainment."

"Good God!" the Duke exclaimed. "Do they never take anything seriously?"

"What seems to me extraordinary," Labby went on, "is that no effort is made to get the useless mouths out of the City. The Duchess will have told you of the vast concentration of animals in the Bois. But I should have thought that it would have made more sense to move people out rather than in."

"So should I," the Duke agreed, "but I suppose the last people anyone is likely to listen to are the English."

"That is certainly true," Henry Labouchere agreed, "and is it essential that the Duchess should not attempt to walk in the streets. Spy-mania has led to situations which are far from comic."

"I have warned Tour," Antonia said, "and he assures me that now when he goes out he wears his oldest clothes and looks more French than the French themselves!"

"You need not worry about Tour," the Duke replied, "but you, Antonia, will stay here with me."

There was an accent on the last word that Antonia did not miss.

After Henry Labouchere had gone, she came back into the Duke's bed-room. He looked at her and said:

"I gather you have a new admirer."

"Shall we say my only . . . admirer," Antonia replied.

The Duke's eyes seemed to rest on her speculatively and she flushed a little under his scrutiny.

He realised that she had lost some weight these past weeks when she had been nursing him, but it had not affected the perfection of her figure.

As he looked at the exquisite line of her breasts, and at the smallness of her waist, he wondered what other young woman would have been content to be cooped up indoors, nursing an unconscious and delirious man, without finding herself restricted or apparently bored.

He raised his eyes to her face and realised she was watching him apprehensively.

Her eyes looked very green because the gown she was wearing was the green of the creeper climbing over the balcony of the bed-room.

It had taken Worth, the Duke thought, to realise that only deep, vivid, or clear colours could make Antonia's skin appear dazzlingly clear and white.

They brought also, both to her eyes and to her hair, strange unpredictable lights that had a fascination all of their own.

He had learnt that Antonia had dismissed her lady's-maid, but he saw that her hair was as elegant and as fashionably arranged as it had been when she had joined him at the Café Anglais and he had not recognised her.

"It is a very dull honeymoon for you, Antonia," he said in his deep voice.

As if she had expected him to say something else, the flush which came to her cheeks seemed to bring an expression of happiness to her face.

"It is at least . . . unusual, and if we are . . . besieged in Paris it might last for a . . . very long time!"

"We must prevent that from happening," the Duke said.

"How can we do that?" Antonia asked.

"By getting out of the City as soon as possible and returning to our own country."

Antonia gave a little cry.

"There is no chance of your moving for weeks! You must not think of it! The Doctor has been very insistent that you must take things very quietly and build up your strength gradually."

"I will not have you put in any danger," the Duke said obstinately.

"How can there possibly be any danger when we are English?" Antonia asked. "I told you, Mr. Labouchere says that English and Americans are pouring into Paris to have a view of the events from the front row of the stalls!"

"He said men were coming," the Duke replied, "not women."

"I shall be safe enough," Antonia insisted, "and have you forgotten that I am not a very feminine woman? In fact you said yourself I am a tom-boy."

"That is the last thing you look at the moment."

Antonia glanced down at her exquisitely made gown.

"If we are going to be here a long time I shall regret that I asked *Monsieur* Worth to deliver to me in England nearly all the garments I had ordered."

"I have a feeling that was a very wise instruction," the Duke said. "For the time being, neither of us will be attending smart Balls or anything that appertains to victory-celebrations."

"At the same time, I want to look nice for you."

"For me or your admirer?" the Duke asked, and there was a sharp note in his voice.

There was a little pause and then he saw the colour rise in Antonia's cheeks.

"For . . . you," she said quietly.

She had the feeling in the days that followed that the Duke was watching her.

She could not understand why sometimes, when she thought he was asleep, she would find in fact that he was awake and that his eyes were on her.

She sat in the window of his room or just outside on the balcony in case he should need anything.

There were fortunately some books in the house and Labby brought her more. She became acquainted with the works of Gustave Flaubert, Victor Hugo, George Sands, Dumas, and many other romantic authors whom she had never had the chance of reading in England.

Sometimes she found that the excitement the written page held for her was interrupted by the feeling she was being watched, and then she would find the Duke's eyes on her.

She wondered to herself if it was in approval or indifference.

She longed to ask him if he missed the Marchioness; but the frankness with which she had been able to talk to him when they had first been married seemed to have vanished since the duel and his long illness.

She knew the answer to that herself, and she only prayed that he would never realise it.

When she had seen him fall to the ground and when she had thought as she reached his side that he was dead, she had known that she loved him.

As she and Tour, assisted by the Duke's seconds, had carried him to the carriage and he had been laid on the back seat, his head in her lap, she admitted that she loved him agonisingly.

She had done so, she thought later, from the first moment when she had gone to his house to ask him if he would marry her rather than Felicity.

How, she asked herself, could any woman have resisted that strange, attractive, mocking expression in his eyes and the faintly cynical twist to his lips?

Now she could understand all too vividly what the Marchioness, the Comtesse, and what doubtless every woman he had met, felt for him.

No wonder, when a whole world of beautiful women could be his, that he did not wish to tie himself to one dull, unattractive girl with no knowledge of anything except horses.

"I love you! I love you!" she whispered to him in the long nights when she nursed him.

He had cried out deliriously, sometimes talking gibberish she could not understand, but at other times speaking of things that had taken place in his life.

Gradually, after questioning Tour, she could understand what had actually happened.

He had fallen from a tree when he was a small boy and very nearly dislocated his neck.

He had been unconscious for a long time and forced to lie on his back so that the injuries he had done to himself would not become permanent.

He had thought in his delirium that it was happening to him again, and as Antonia had held him in her arms, he had cried out for his mother.

When she tried to prevent him from throwing himself about in case he should injure the wound in his chest, Antonia had felt as if she were his mother and he were her child.

"You are all right, darling," she had murmured to him. "You are safe. You will not fall again; see, I am holding you close against me, and you cannot fall."

She felt gradually that her voice got through to him and that he understood.

Then he would turn his head against her breast as if seeking the comfort which only she could give him. She knew, at these times, that she loved him with her whole being as she had never thought she could love anybody.

Another night the Duke had thought he had had a fall while hunting. When Antonia questioned Tour, he remembered when he had broken his collar-bone and it had been very painful for some time.

He had cried out then for someone, but Antonia suspected that although he mentioned no name, it was not his mother he sought but another woman who he imagined would comfort him.

"It was not possible for me to be in his thoughts," Antonia told herself, "but lucky I am that he should turn to me and need me as I have never been needed before."

Gradually, as her love grew within her day after day, she understood that this was what she had always wanted, someone to love, someone to whom she was important and not just a nuisance and an irritation.

Someone she could also care for not only physically but with her whole heart.

'Even if he does not love me,' Antonia thought, 'I can love him. But he must never know of it!'

Sometimes now when the Duke was asleep she would creep to his bed-side to look at him. Then she would feel that her breasts ached because she could not hold him anymore in her arms and know that he would turn to her like an unhappy child.

She decided that when the Duke was well enough she would ask him to give her a baby. It would be a part of him which she could love and she was no longer afraid of the idea.

She thought of how foolish she had been not to let him make her his wife the first night they were married.

She wondered now why she had ever thought it important that they should get to know each other first. What really mattered was that she could have given him the heir he wanted and she would have had his child to love.

"When we get back to England," she told herself, "he will go back to the Marchioness, but nothing and nobody can take this time away from me! He is mine . . . mine now, and there is no other woman to distract him."

She felt herself quiver with a sudden ecstasy as she whispered:

"I have held him in my arms and . . . kissed his cheek . . . his forehead, and his . . . hair."

She schooled herself in the day-time to be very circumspect, so that the Duke would not suspect for one moment how much it had thrilled her when he asked her to lift him up against his pillows, to arrange them behind his head.

She even found herself, as the Duke got better, growing jealous of Tour because he asked so much more from him than he did from her.

She wanted to serve him, she wanted to be useful to him.

But when she had made him well, she remembered, he would make love to the Marchioness!

She felt the pain of it strike at her like a dagger in her heart.

Chapter Six

"How are you feeling?" Antonia asked.

"Well enough to go home," the Duke replied.

He was sitting in an armchair in the window, and Antonia looking at him thought that he did in fact seem much better.

At the same time, both she and Tour knew that he was still far from being himself.

Thanks to Labby, who had found a Chinese masseur, the Duke was in fact not as weak in the body as he might have been after such a long time in bed.

At the same time, Antonia knew it would be a great mistake, at this stage in his convalescence, to over-tax his strength.

There were, however, many more difficulties arising from the situation in Paris than they had dared relate to the Duke, because they knew it would worry him.

They had not even told him that the Germans were approaching nearer and nearer day by day.

"We are British," he said, "so there is no need to think that we cannot leave whenever we might wish to do so."

Antonia hesitated. He had given her an answer, and now she had the reply:

"We are, as a Nation, very unpopular."

"Why?" the Duke enquired.

"According to Mr. Labouchere, French opinion has been scandalised by the unfriendly attitude of the British Press."

The Duke made an exasperated sound which she knew meant he thought little of the Press one way or another.

"Once Paris was threatened," she went on, "it was widely assumed that Britain would enter the lists to rescue the Fount of Civilisation."

She paused before saying with a nervous note in her voice:

"Now, the feeling against us is so intense that *Les Nouvelles* even proposed that all the British in Paris should be shot at once!"

"Good Heavens!" the Duke exclaimed.

"When the street names of Paris were changed after the fall of the Empire," Antonia went on, "the French Press demanded that the Rue de Londres should be renamed on the grounds that the name of Londres was detested even more than Berlin."

"I cannot believe this is any more than gutter journalism," the Duke said sharply. "I shall myself call at the British Embassy tomorrow!"

Antonia said nothing for a moment and then changing the subject she asked:

"I can see you have a headache. Will you let me massage your forehead? You know it helps you."

She hoped as she spoke that she did not sound too eager. To touch the Duke was such a delight that she found it difficult to hide her feelings in case he should guess how much she loved him.

"Perhaps it will help," he said a little grudgingly.

She rose to stand behind his chair and placed her two hands very gently on his forehead, soothing away the tension in a way he remembered her doing when he had been ill.

"How did you learn to do this?" he asked.

"Ives found that it helped your horses when they had a sprained fetlock," Antonia replied.

The Duke gave a short laugh.

"I might have guessed it was connected with horses!"

"I do not think I should have been allowed to practise on a man," Antonia said with a little smile.

"I am grateful that I can be the first in that field, at any rate," the Duke remarked.

There was a slightly cynical and mocking note in his voice, and she wondered why.

Recently he had seemed almost to resent her attentions—or perhaps that was not the right word. It was as if he challenged her in some way which she could not understand.

"We must get away," he said suddenly. "We must get back to England and a normal life. I am sure that is what you want as much as I do."

With difficulty Antonia prevented herself from crying out that it was the last thing she wanted.

"Or perhaps," the Duke went on, as if he was following the train of his own thoughts, "you would rather be here, receiving the attentions of your journalist admirer."

"Mr. Labouchere has been very kind," Antonia said, "and when you are ready to leave I know he will help us."

"I very much doubt if I shall need his help," the Duke said loftily. "As I have already told you, I will go to the British Embassy tomorrow and arrange with Lord Lyon, our Ambassador, our safe conveyance to Le Havre, where the yacht will be waiting."

"You must be quite strong enough before we undertake the journey," Antonia insisted.

"I intend to walk in the garden after I have rested this afternoon," the Duke said, "and my masseur assures me that my muscles are in perfect trim. It is just a question of not reopening the wound on my shoulder."

He did not add, Antonia noticed, that each time he got up out of bed he felt rather dizzy.

He resented any form of weakness, fighting against it with a determination which in part was the reason why he had recovered so quickly.

At the same time, she knew that once they returned to England she would lose him, and she wished that whatever might happen in Paris they could stay on at least for a little while.

The Duke was resting after luncheon, at which he had eaten quite a decent meal, having no idea how difficult it had been to procure, when the manservant announced that *Monsieur* Labouchere was in the Salon.

Antonia went in to him and he lifted her hand to his lips, holding it longer than necessary and looking at her in a manner which made her feel shy.

"You look a little tired," he said in concern. "Are you still nursing your importunate invalid at night?"

"No, of course not," Antonia replied. "I sleep peacefully and my husband has a bell that he rings if he requires anything. He has not awakened me for several nights now."

"Yet subconsciously you listen for it," Labby said perceptively.

Antonia smiled.

"You are not to worry about me. My husband wishes to go home."

"He told me so yesterday," Labby replied. "It is not going to be easy."

"He says that he will see the British Ambassador tomorrow."

"That will be impossible," Labby answered. "He left this morning with the last of the British Corps Diplomatique."

"I do not believe it!" Antonia exclaimed.

"I am afraid it is the truth," Labby replied. "I was told that had happened, and because I was thinking about you I called at the Embassy on my way here."

Antonia drew in her breath as he went on:

"There is no Official left now in the British Embassy, save a concierge whose duty, I gather, is to shrug his shoulders to all enquiries and say, parrot-wise, 'I cannot give you any information.'"

"I have never heard of anything so extraordinary!" Antonia exclaimed. "I thought the British Ambassador would stay as long as there were any English in Paris."

"There are some four thousand still in the City," Labby told her.

"If the Ambassador has gone, then I feel we should go too," Antonia said in a frightened voice. "Are there any trains running?"

"I think it unlikely you will be able to get on one even if there were."

Labby paused and Antonia knew that he was keeping something from her.

"Tell me the truth," she begged.

"I have only just learnt that a train which left the Gare du Nord on September fifteenth was seized by Prussian out-riders at Senlis, which you know is only twenty-seven miles north of Paris."

Antonia gasped but did not speak, and Labby went on:

"I think it was that which must have persuaded Lord Lyon and the British Consul to leave this morning."

"Why did the French Government not insist on all the British leaving earlier?" Antonia asked despairingly.

"The Government and the Council of National Defence has said that large groups of foreigners leaving the City would be . . . demoralising to the Army and the citizens."

"But we are nothing but useless mouths," Antonia persisted.

"That is what a number of British have already said to me," Labby replied, "but I can assure you, the French Government will not listen, and in my opinion they are making a mess of everything."

He spoke almost savagely and then said:

"I will get you away somehow, I promise you that. At the same time, if I followed my own wishes, I would keep you here."

Antonia glanced at him enquiringly and saw the look in his eyes and quickly looked away.

"I love you, Antonia," he said very quietly. "You know that by this time."

"You must not . . . say such . . . things."

"What harm can it do?" he asked. "I know what your feelings are where I am concerned."

He gave a sigh which seemed to come from the very depths of his being as he said:

"I realise that I am much too old for you. Had I been ten years younger I would have done my damnedest to seduce you. As it is, I will leave you as I found you, perfect and unspoilt—perhaps, in a long list of conquests, the only woman I have ever really loved."

There was something in Labby's voice which made Antonia feel curiously near to tears.

There was nothing she could say. She was only perturbed that she should have brought unhappiness to someone who had been so kind.

As if he knew what she was thinking, Labby went on:

"Perhaps one day when you are older you will understand how difficult it has been these past weeks, when we have been so much alone together, for me to behave with an unaccustomed constraint and control."

"It has meant so . . . much to me to have your . . . friendship," Antonia faltered.

"It is not friendship, Antonia," Labby contradicted, "it is love! A love so different from anything I have known or felt in the past that sometimes I think I must be dreaming and you do not really exist, except in my imagination."

"You should not talk to me like . . . this, as you . . . well know," Antonia said.

But she wondered even as she spoke why she should prevent him from doing so.

The Duke would not care if another man made love to her. After all, he was in love with the Marchioness. When they returned to England she would have nobody in her life, neither the man she loved nor the man who loved her.

She had half turned away, and Labby, as he was speaking, put his hands on her shoulders to turn her round to face him.

"What is it about you that is so different from other

women?" he asked. "You are not outstandingly beautiful, and yet I cannot be free of the fascination of your
face."

She saw the pain in his eyes as he went on:

"I hear your voice in my ears, your figure makes
any other woman look coarse and ungainly, and I find
it almost impossible to think of anyone else but you."

There was a depth of passion in his tone which made
Antonia feel shy and a little afraid.

Then he released her and walked across the Salon to
stand at the window looking into the garden.

"When you leave," he said, "all I shall have are my
dreams. I have the uncomfortable feeling that they will
haunt me for the rest of my life."

Antonia made a little helpless gesture.

"What can I . . . say?" she asked. "You know I do
not wish to . . . hurt you."

"It is banal to say, 'it is better to have loved and lost
than never to have loved at all,' " Labby replied in the
tone of a man mocking himself. "In my case, it happens to be true. You have done a wonderful thing for
me, my sweet Duchess."

"What is that?" Antonia asked.

"You have restored my faith in women. I have
watched the manner in which they defamed and prosti-
tuted in every possible way the Second Empire. I saw
their greed, their hypocrisy, their perfidy! You have
shown me that women can be pure and faithful, true
and uncorrupted."

He gave her one of his cynical smiles as he said:

"I have always thought that each woman a man
loves leaves a tombstone in his life. On yours will be
written—'She gave me faith.' "

"Thank you, Labby," Antonia said very softly.

Then without waiting for him to say good-bye she
went from the Salon and left him alone.

*   *   *

"I do not believe you!" the Duke ejaculated angrily.

"It is true," Henry Labouchere replied. "The Uhlans
from two Prussian Armies joined hands yesterday, Sep-

tember twentieth, near Versailles, which surrendered without a shot."

There was silence for a moment. Then the Duke said:

"That means that Paris is now severed from the rest of France. I can hardly believe it!"

"What do the people feel?" Antonia asked.

"At the moment the mood is 'Let them come, let the cannon thunder! It has been too long!' " Labby replied. "But retribution has been enacted violently upon the wretched deserters."

"If they desert, they deserve all they get!" the Duke said in a hard voice.

"I cannot help being sorry for them," Labby answered. "According to reports, they were not only badly led, but many of them were without arms. The young Zouaves panicked the first time they were shelled by a well-trained Prussian field-gun battery."

"What is happening to them now?" Antonia enquired.

"Montmartre is full of them and an angry mob was spitting in their faces and threatening to lynch them until the *Garde Nationale* escorted them with many prods of their rifle-butts into the centre of the City."

"And what else is taking place?" the Duke enquired.

"The great difficulty is going to be to get news out of the City," Labby replied. "A possible solution may be balloons."

"Balloons!" the Duke exclaimed in surprise.

"A number have been located," Labby replied, "unfortunately, most of them in various states of disrepair. It is, however, an idea, though not where passengers are concerned."

"I was not thinking we should fly from Paris!" the Duke said sharply. "What I am considering is whether it could be any use appealing to the French to negotiate with the Germans for a special pass."

"I thought of that," Labby answered. "The Duchess has already requested me to find some way in which you could leave."

"Is it possible?" the Duke enquired.

"This morning I watched four Britons, who I happened to know, climbing gaily into a carriage loaded with hampers of provisions, luggage, and with an English flag flying."

"What happened?" the Duke asked.

"They got as far as Pont de Neuilly, where they were seized and taken before General Ducrot. He said to them, 'I cannot understand you English: If you want to get shot, we will shoot you ourselves to save you trouble.'"

Labby paused for a moment and then went on:

"My friends swear they will try again tomorrow, but I should think it unlikely they will get through."

"Then what can we do?" the Duke asked.

"Give me a little time," Labby begged. "The Prussians are bringing up their big guns. The bombardment will not start yet."

Antonia looked frightened.

"You think they will bombard us?"

"Naturally," Labby replied. "It is the obvious thing to do if they want a quick surrender."

That night, Antonia lay awake wondering if she would hear the shells thudding and exploding in the centre of the City, but everything was quiet and she thought that perhaps Labby had exaggerated the danger.

There was however no doubt that the Duke took him seriously and in the next few days he became more and more restless.

He was only prevented with difficulty from going out of the house to see for himself what was occurring.

It was Antonia who finally managed to dissuade him by saying she would be frightened if she were left alone.

"I cannot stay here like a caged animal," the Duke said irritably.

"S-suppose you were . . . killed, or . . . arrested," Antonia said. "What would happen to . . . me?"

It was an unanswerable argument, and the Duke had listened to Labouchere when he said that if he went to the French authorities and declared who he was, they could take two courses of action.

They might consider an English Duke so important that they would give him no chance of ever leaving Paris, in case he fell into the hands of the Prussians.

"Or else," Labby went on, "they will arrest you on some trumped-up charge merely to force the British Government to pay more attention to the Siege of Paris!"

Both, the Duke realised, were quite viable arguments, but he was now more determined than ever that they must leave Paris somehow without anybody realising who they were.

However, when he had suffered nearly a week's inactivity, while getting stronger day by day, he said to Antonia:

"You know I would not wish deliberately to take you into danger, but I am quite convinced that the Siege is going to get very much worse before the French surrender."

"You think they really will surrender?" Antonia asked in surprise. "Surely someone will come to their rescue."

"Who is likely to do so?" the Duke asked, and she knew there was no answer.

"But if Paris holds out without relief from outside, the Siege might last indefinitely."

"It can only last as long as there is enough food to eat," the Duke replied.

"But surely there will be enough for a very long time?"

Antonia thought as she spoke of all the animals in the Bois.

"Tour has told me," the Duke replied, "that people are talking, if things get really bad, of slaughtering the animals in the Zoo. And there is no doubt that cats and dogs will be in danger of their lives as soon as what meat is obtainable in the butchers' shops is priced beyond the purse of the very poor!"

Antonia gave a little cry.

"I cannot bear to think of it."

"Nor can I where you are concerned," the Duke said. "And that is why I have to decide whether it would be best to risk our being caught or shot by the Prussians outside Paris, or to stop here and starve, as undoubtedly the Parisians will do eventually."

Antonia did not hesitate.

"I know what you would prefer," she said, "and I am prepared to take any risk that you wish."

"Thank you, Antonia," the Duke said. "I knew I could rely on you to show courage."

He smiled at her in a way she found irresistible as he added:

"Perhaps it will be no more frightening and no more dangerous than leaping over the high hedges and the Water-Jump on The Chase!"

* * *

The soldiers guarding the Porte de St. Cloud watched a wooden cart trundling towards them, drawn by a frisky young mule.

It was driven by a woman muffled in shawls, despite the heat, and with a dirty cotton handkerchief tied under her chin.

As the cart drew near to the gate she began to cry out loudly and defiantly:

"*La Vérole!*"

"*Danger!*"

"*Contagieuse!*"

The Corporal in front of the gate held up his hand and with a little difficulty she drew the mule to a standstill.

"What is all this?" he asked.

"*La Vérole*," she replied, jerking her thumb backwards to where he could now see a man lying on the straw of the wooden cart.

"Smallpox!"

The Corporal took a step backwards.

"I have my papers if you want to see them," the woman said, speaking in an argot, "but I should be careful how you touch them."

She held them out to the soldier, who made no effort to take them.

"Where do you think you are going, *Madame?*"

"We've been turned out," she answered. "There's not a man amongst the sniffling cowards in this City who'll touch a smallpox case as bad as his!"

Without moving his feet, the Corporal peered over the edge of the cart. He could see that the face of the man lying on the straw was covered with flaming-red pock-marks and shuddered.

"Go on, get out of here!" he said harshly, "and the quicker the better!"

The woman whipped the mule, the gate was opened, and they proceeded until they came to the Prussian outpost just outside the town of St. Cloud.

Here the same explanation was given, but the papers signed by the Doctor were inspected and there was some delay while a junior Officer was produced.

"The man you are conveying, *Madame,*" he said in guttural but just intelligible French, "may have smallpox, but that is no reason why you should leave the City with him."

She did not answer, but pulled back a ragged cuff that covered her wrist. On her skin he could see two flaming-red pock-marks! Hastily he handed her back the papers.

"Go away as far as you can from Paris," he ordered.

"We're going to Mantes, *Mein Herr,*" the woman said. "That's if we reach it before we die!"

The German Officer was, however, not listening, as he hurried away to wash his hands after touching her papers. The soldiers watched them go with a look of relief on their smileless faces, and one of them said:

"I would rather die from a bullet than that disease."

"For such filth it would be a waste of ammunition," the other answered.

Antonia's back was very straight as she drove away, and it was an effort not to look behind her.

She touched the mule with her whip and made him go faster. Only when the Prussian out-post was out of

sight did the Duke sit up from the floor of the wooden
cart and say:

"I am being rattled to bits!"

"You can come up here and drive," Antonia replied
over her shoulder.

"It is certainly what I would prefer," he answered.

Antonia slackened the speed of the mule a little, but
she did not pull up to a stand-still.

The Duke climbed into the front of the cart and took
the reins from her.

"Is it safe to wipe this blasted paint off my face?" he
asked.

"I should leave it for the moment," she replied.
"There will be, as Labby warned us, Germans all over
the place, and whatever happens, we must not get
captured."

"I am aware of that," he said, "but according to reports, they have not yet reached Amiens."

"Can we trust the reports?"

"Tour will get to Le Havre all right," the Duke said.

The valet had left two days earlier in the company of
some Americans who had managed by some extraordinary good luck to obtain permits both from the
French and the Germans.

There had been no chance, however, even if they had
wished to do so, of taking anyone extra with them. The
pass was merely for themselves and their servants.

Only by bribing the American's French servant with
what seemed to Antonia an almost astronomical
amount of francs had Tour persuaded the man to stay
in Paris while he took his place.

Once Henry Labouchere and the Duke had worked
out a plan of campaign, they had instructed Tour down
to the minutest detail as to what he should do.

Horses were to be left for Antonia and the Duke at
a village which Labby was certain was not at the moment under Prussian occupation.

"Buy the best you can," the Duke said, "and then
hire the fastest conveyance that is obtainable and get
to Le Havre where the yacht will be waiting."

"The Prussians will not touch a British ship," Labby had said firmly.

"No, but they might prevent us boarding her," the Duke replied, "and that is why if Le Havre is under Prussian occupation, Tour must somehow get in touch with my Captain and tell him to take the yacht to Cherbourg."

"It is much, much further," Antonia said nervously.

"I know that," the Duke said, "but I intend to take no risks where you are concerned. Somehow, if it is necessary, we will make our way across country, and we may be lucky."

"The reports at the moment," Labby told them, "but of course they are not completely reliable, are that the Prussians have not advanced, at least in any strength, further than St. Quentin."

"In which case Versailles and Évreux will be all right," the Duke said, "but I do not intend to visit any towns. We will keep to the fields and we may find something to eat in the small villages."

"Having seen the way the people were behaving in Paris, Your Grace," Tour said, "I should not rely on it. If they have any food, I am quite certain that the French, when they fear that they themselves might go hungry, will not give away or even sell anything that is edible to passing travellers."

"I am afraid that may be true," Labby agreed. "Hundreds of stragglers have brought the Army into disrepute with the locals. I am told French farmers have barred their doors and threatened to fire on the starving troops begging for food."

"We will take what we can with us," Antonia said quietly. "Otherwise, we shall just have to be hungry for a day or two until we reach the yacht."

As she spoke she felt worried not for herself, but for the Duke.

He was much better, but she knew this journey would be a tremendous strain and she wondered what she would do if he collapsed, perhaps in some hostile French village where there would be no Doctor.

But when they set off the Duke was in good spirits simply because he was at last being active.

He had laughed at the clothes that Labby had bought for them as a disguise, and when he saw the wooden cart and the mule that was to carry them from Paris he had said to Antonia:

"I am sure, Your Grace, you will find this as impressive, though perhaps not so fast, as the Phaeton in which we set out on our honeymoon."

"I only wish Rufus were drawing it!" Antonia replied.

"So do I," he said quietly.

She had felt a sudden warmth within her because they were sharing their love of horses and a secret which was their own.

But when they had driven away from the house, leaving Labby staring after them with an expression of despair in his eyes, Antonia felt frightened.

It would be bad enough if the French penetrated their disguise, but what if the Prussians did!

She felt herself tremble at what might happen, knowing that it would be hard to explain who they were or to get anyone to believe them.

Then she told herself that whatever happened, she was with the Duke.

The secret island on which they existed in a strange unreal world had now been left behind. They were crossing the hostile sea which she had sensed was always waiting for them outside.

But she told herself almost despairingly that, while the Duke would be travelling to safety and to England, she was returning to loneliness, to being unwanted as she had been all her life.

Once he was back with the Marchioness, there would be no-one for her to look after, to comfort, to sustain.

Perhaps sometimes, she told herself, he would want her to massage his forehead.

Perhaps because they had been through so much together there would be things to talk about which other women could not share.

But when she thought of the Marchioness's beauty, she knew that even a Worth gown could not make her look like a fairy on a Christmas-tree, or have the unbelievable loveliness of the woman who called in uninvited to see them the first night they were married.

"It is hopeless!" Antonia told herself.

At the same time, there were two, perhaps three, days left when she would be alone with the Duke!

Even to sit beside him in the front of the cart, realising how grotesque they both looked in their ragged clothes, the Duke's face painted with smallpox eruptions, was still an indescribable thrill.

The village where Tour was to leave the horses for them was ten miles out of Paris and off the beaten track.

They left the main road for a dusty and twisting lane.

Antonia realised with relief that they were getting into an uninhabited part of the country where there were thick forests and only occasional small and unimportant hamlets.

Labby had suggested they should leave by Porte de St. Cloud because the Prussian lines of investment were nearer to Paris there than at any other place.

"The sooner you are away from the City and its environment, the better. There is always the chance that you might encounter some officious French Official who would turn you back. And whatever you do, keep north when you are through the German lines, otherwise you will find yourself in Versailles, which is full of Uhlans."

"Do you think we are going in the right direction?" Antonia asked the Duke tentatively.

"I have a good bump of location," he answered, "and I have studied the map very carefully. Once we have found the horses, we should have an uninterrupted ride across country."

He spoke in a calm, matter-of-fact manner. Then he said:

"You are not frightened, Antonia?"

"No . . . no," she answered, "not . . . when I am with . . . you."

He looked down at her muffled in her ragged shawls and said with a hint of laughter in his voice:

"I have said it before: this is an incredible honeymoon."

"It will be something to tell our grandchildren," Antonia replied.

Even as she spoke she realised she had assumed that they would have grandchildren, and that entailed first having children.

The Duke did not say anything and merely drove on, keeping the mule at a steady pace and handling the reins with an expertise that he would have shown towards his own superb horses.

They came upon the village unexpectedly at a turn of the road and the Duke drew to a stand-still.

"Is it . . . safe?" Antonia asked.

"I am just making certain that everything is quiet and there is no sign of any Prussians. If there is anything suspicious I will lie down in the back of the cart. It is always best to be prepared, Antonia, and not to take risks."

"Yes, of course," she said, "you think of everything."

"I am thinking of you," he said sharply.

But she wondered if in fact he was resenting that he must look after a woman instead of being able to forge ahead and hurry back to England.

She was well aware that if she had not been with him he would have left several days earlier.

It was not because he doubted his own strength that he had listened to her pleadings and to Labby's good common sense, but because he realised that having Antonia with him was an added responsibility.

The village appeared quiet and safe in the morning sunshine.

The Duke approached a small Inn, called Le Coq d'Or.

He drove the mule into the yard and handed Antonia the reins.

Then jumping down from the cart, he went to the pump in the centre of the yard and washed his face.

'It may be taking a risk,' Antonia thought, 'but it would certainly be unwise to frighten the French who are holding the horses for us.'

She slipped the papers, which they had used to escape through the barriers, down the front of her dress.

Then as the Duke disappeared into the Inn she climbed down from the cart and went to the mule, patting his neck and talking to him in a voice which all horses seem to understand whatever their nationality.

The Duke came back with a thick-set elderly man who, Antonia guessed, was the proprietor of the Inn.

She noticed that the Duke had removed the ragged garments which he had been wearing over his riding-clothes, except that he still had on his feet a pair of disreputable, toe-less shoes.

Antonia burrowed in the straw and produced his riding-boots.

Then as she heard the two men talking inside the stable she took off the shawls and the full, ragged skirt which covered her own riding-habit.

It was very elegant because she had not thought to bring with her the one she had bought in London, knowing it would be far too severe to be worn riding in the Bois.

Instead, she had on a habit of thin piqué which the Empress had made all the vogue and in which Worth had dressed all the fashionable Courtesans as well as the Ladies of Quality.

The only thing Antonia had not dared to bring with her was her riding-hat, but she had a scarf of the same colour as her riding-habit with which she could cover her hair.

She was, however, aware that her hair must look lamentable without the fashionable coiffure which had done so much to change her appearance from that of a dowdy English bride to that of the *chic* woman with whom Labby had fallen in love.

Realising the mule had found some grass to eat amongst the weeds growing in the court-yard, she left him and went into the Inn.

A woman, whom she guessed to be the wife of the proprietor, was very willing to show her upstairs to a poorly furnished bed-room, where, however, she could wash and there was a mirror in which she could arrange her hair.

She was as quick as she could be because she was quite certain the Duke would wish to get away. In a few minutes she was at least more presentable and had arranged the gauze scarf over her up-swept hair before she hurried downstairs.

As she had expected, she found the Duke waiting for her impatiently. The horses were saddled and Antonia saw that Tour had managed to procure a side-saddle for her.

They were rough-looking not particularly prepossessing beasts, but she realised they were sturdy and would undoubtedly endure the long journey better than well-bred and faster animals.

The Duke had a glass of wine in his hand and the proprietor handed one to Antonia.

She was just about to protest that she did not need anything alcoholic to drink, when she thought that the Duke had ordered it for her, and it might be a long time before they would get anything else to drink.

This idea, however, was dispelled when the proprietor said:

"I put the food the gentleman ordered for you, *Monsieur,* in the saddle-bag, and there are two bottles of wine in *Madame*'s."

"Thank you again," the Duke said, "I am extremely grateful."

He tipped the man and helped Antonia onto her saddle.

For a moment she was close to him, his hands were touching her, and she felt a thrill like quicksilver run through her.

Then the Duke had mounted his own horse, and without speaking they rode from the Inn, through the small village, and out into the open country.

"So far so good, Antonia," the Duke said with a note

of satisfaction in his voice, after they had travelled some way.

"Tour has obviously got through."

"And so have we." The Duke smiled. "As you said just now, Antonia, this is a story that will undoubtedly enthrall our children."

He did not look at her as he spoke but Antonia felt the colour rise in her cheeks.

"Please God, let him give me . . . a child," she prayed in her heart. "I love him . . . I love him so desperately."

Chapter Seven

Antonia thought she was lying on a soft cloud. She felt as if she were sinking into it deeper and deeper until it enveloped her whole body.

Then gradually she became aware that everything was very quiet and there was in fact a pillow under her head.

Slowly her mind began to work and she realised she had been asleep for a very long time. She opened her eyes slowly, as if she were afraid, until as she saw the outline of the cabin she knew where she was.

She was on the yacht, they had reached safety, they had won!

Antonia turned over onto her side and could not remember coming aboard. She could recall the moment when they had arrived at the Quay at Le Havre and seen the Duke's yacht at anchor, gleaming white against the blue of the waves.

She had stood staring at it, feeling, now that she no longer had the support of her horse, that if she moved she would fall down from sheer exhaustion.

Vaguely she had recalled someone helping her into a boat, then she must have fallen asleep.

"How is it I can remember nothing of what happened next?" she asked herself, and saw that her arm was naked.

She moved the blanket which covered her and realised someone had removed her riding-habit.

She was wearing only her full petticoats and a silk

chemise. Even the waist of the petticoat had been undone so that she would not be restricted.

She knew who must have undressed her and felt herself blush at the thought.

How could she not have known that he was touching her?

Perhaps he had carried her to her cabin; but she had been so tired, so utterly and completely exhausted, that everything had been swept away in her need for sleep.

Even the first day had been tiring, because she had not been riding for nearly two months. But she had been too preoccupied in worrying about the Duke to think of herself.

They had ridden hard and said very little. Watching him, however, Antonia knew that he was tense every time they saw people in the distance, or were in sight of a main road.

The highways seemed unaccountably crowded, although whether it was with Germans, stragglers from the French Army, or refugees, Antonia had no idea.

She guessed that the Duke was as apprehensive of meeting French deserters who were living off the land as he was of encountering the invaders.

'They would rob us,' Antonia thought, 'and would undoubtedly take our horses.'

She understood why the Duke skirted even the smallest hamlets and kept to the open fields.

They stopped for a very short while to eat some of the food which Tour had ordered for them. There was crisp French bread, a rough local pâté, cheese, and fruit, which they finished the first day.

It seemed delicious, but by dinner-time they both were too tired to feel hungry and were only grateful for being able to drink a little wine from the bottles in Antonia's saddle-bag.

It was nearly dusk when the Duke reined in his horse, which was now moving much more slowly than it had done before, and said:

"We must find somewhere to sleep, Antonia, but I am afraid your accommodation for tonight must be in a wood."

"I think I would sleep on top of a mountain and on bare rocks at this moment." Antonia smiled.

"You are tired?" he asked sharply.

"Very," she replied truthfully, "and so are you."

She had in fact been worrying about him for several hours, aware that he was over-taxing his strength.

But knowing too that as he concentrated on getting them away, he would not acknowledge his own weakness or the fact that his wound was doubtlessly hurting him.

They stopped in a small wood surrounded by open fields which would make it, if they were watching out, impossible for anyone to approach them unawares.

Having unsaddled the horses and made quite certain they could not wander away, the Duke flung himself down on the moss-covered ground beside Antonia and she saw the lines of fatigue on his face.

"If you will put your head in my lap," she suggested tentatively after they had finished eating, "I will massage your forehead."

"You will do nothing of the sort, Antonia!" the Duke replied. "You will lie close to me and go to sleep. I want to leave here at dawn."

Thinking there was no point in arguing, Antonia did as she was told.

After he had moved restlessly for several minutes as if he were in pain, she knew by his even breathing that he was fast asleep.

Very, very carefully, she moved herself a little higher up the soft ground so that she could put her arm beneath his head and hold him close against her breast.

'This may be for the last time,' she thought. 'I may never be able to do this again.'

Very gently she massaged his forehead with the soothing strokes she had used when he was delirious.

As she did so she felt him relax, and knew that he was sleeping deeply, too deeply for her to awaken him inadvertently.

It was then that she kissed his hair, telling him wordlessly how much she loved him.

'I love you! Oh, my darling . . . I love you!'

She held him closer still, his head heavy against her, and she thought that for the moment she had never been so happy.

"I must move away," she told herself, "before I fall asleep. . . ."

*   *   *

The next thing Antonia knew was that the Duke was calling her. He was already up and had saddled both the horses.

Hurriedly she got the food and wine ready for them to have a scanty breakfast before they set out again.

The bread was stale by now and not very appetising, but it was not a moment to be fastidious.

The next day was very much like the first and Antonia knew that Tour's choice of their horses had been a wise one.

Like their riders, they might be tired, but they kept going at a fair pace and Antonia knew that the miles between them and Le Havre were lessening every hour.

"Do you know where we are?" she asked the Duke once.

"I have a good idea," he replied briefly.

He obviously did not want to talk, and Antonia was silent, knowing that as they rode the Duke was always on the alert for any unexpected danger.

They stopped a little earlier than they had the night before, simply because both they and the horses found it difficult to go any further.

The heat of the day had changed when the sky became overcast and a chill wind began to blow across the open countryside.

For the first time Antonia wished that her smart piqué habit was more substantial, and that she had not thrown away all the shawls in which she had disguised herself for leaving Paris.

She did not complain, but the Duke must have known what she was feeling because a mile later he said:

"I see a barn ahead. If, as it appears, it is not connected to a farm-house, I think that is where we will stay the night."

The barn was in fact some distance from the farm-house which lay about a quarter of a mile away.

What was more, it was half full with hay, which provided not only fodder for the horses but a comfortable resting-place for two very tired people.

They ate a little of the dry bread and the pâté, which still tasted quite pleasant, although rather monotonous. Then Antonia sank down into the hay.

"I would not change this," she said, "at the moment for the most comfortable mattress in Doncaster Park!"

The Duke picked up some handfuls of hay and covered her with it.

"This will keep you warm just as effectively as a woollen blanket," he said. "I should have thought to suggest that you brought a riding-cloak with you."

"I should have thought of it myself," Antonia replied, "but it was so hot in Paris."

"I think it is going to rain."

The Duke lay down on the hay and they neither of them heard the rain pouring down in the night.

But when they left the barn in the morning the earth felt fresh and the horses seemed to respond to the coolness in the air.

They stopped to water the animals at the first stream and then they were off again.

Antonia hoped and prayed that they would reach the end of their journey before nightfall. She would not have admitted it to the Duke, but her body was feeling very stiff and the saddle was not a comfortable one.

The day seemed unaccountably long, but she knew hopefully that the end was near when the Duke insisted on her drinking quite a lot of the last bottle of wine and then threw it away.

"Only a few more hours," he said encouragingly.

"You can manage?" Antonia asked anxiously.

"I am worrying about you and not myself!" the Duke answered.

"That is ridiculous!" she protested. "You are the invalid."

She knew as she spoke that she had said the wrong thing.

"I am nothing of the sort, Antonia," he said almost sharply, "and this would be a taxing journey for any woman, even an Amazon like yourself."

He was teasing her and she felt happy because he was well enough to do so.

As the hours dragged by she grew tireder and tireder.

Fortunately, the horses kept together and when she thought the Duke was not watching her she was able to hold on to the pommel of her saddle.

"I must not fail him now," she kept telling herself. "We have got so far. I cannot let him down at the very last moment."

But the very last moment seemed far away and when finally they clattered over the cobbled streets of Le Havre she thought that if a whole battalion of Prussian soldiers was waiting for them she would be unable to make any effort to escape.

Now she made no pretence of not holding on to the pommel with both hands, and the Duke reached out to take the bridle of her horse as they rode down to the Quay.

She had heard him giving orders; she felt him lift her down from the saddle and help her into a boat. Then there was a blank.

"He should have been the one to collapse, not me," Antonia told herself, and was ashamed that she had so little fortitude.

She wondered what time it was and even as she thought about it, the door of the cabin opened very softly and she knew someone was peeping inside.

"I am . . . awake!" she said, and her voice sounded hoarse and strange.

"I thought you might be, Your Grace."

Tour came into the cabin and pulled back the curtains over the port-holes.

"We are safe!" Antonia exclaimed.

"You are indeed, Your Grace. There are no dangers in Southampton Harbour."

"Southampton!" Antonia queried. "But how can we have got here so quickly?"

Tour smiled.

"You slept all of yesterday, Your Grace, in fact you have been asleep for two nights and a whole day, and it is now nearly noon!"

"I cannot believe it!" Antonia exclaimed. "And His Grace?"

She waited apprehensively in case Tour should tell her the Duke was ill.

"His Grace also slept the whole way over. He had a little dinner last night and went straight back to sleep."

"He is all right?" Antonia enquired.

"Fit as a fiddle, Your Grace. There is no need to worry about him."

"And the journey did not hurt his wound?"

"It appears to me not to have changed in any way since I last saw it in Paris."

"Thank God for that!" Antonia exclaimed.

"And thank God you and His Grace arrived safely," Tour said solemnly.

"And you," Antonia added. "Was it a difficult journey?"

"It had its unpleasant moments, but I will tell Your Grace about them another time."

He bent down as he spoke and Antonia saw him pick up her dusty, travel-stained riding-habit which lay on the floor.

"I expect Your Grace would like a bath," he said, "and I have some good news for you."

"What is it?" Antonia asked.

"When I came aboard I found that when six weeks ago *Monsieur* Worth passed through Le Havre on his way to England, he saw the yacht in the Harbour and asked to whom it belonged."

Tour paused to make what he had to say even more dramatic.

"When he learnt it belonged to His Grace, he sent aboard the trunks in which he was conveying Your Grace's purchases to England."

"Oh, Tour, I cannot believe it!" Antonia cried. "How wonderful! Bring me my bath, and then I will make myself look respectable for His Grace."

"His Grace has gone ashore, so there is no hurry," Tour replied. "First I must get Your Grace something to eat."

Antonia smiled.

"As you mention it," she said, "I do feel ravenously hungry."

She ate what seemed to her an enormous amount of eggs and bacon, while Tour filled her bath with hot water and brought into the cabin one of the trunks that *Monsieur* Worth had left for her.

There was a fascinating choice of garments, but knowing it was likely to be colder in England than it had been in Paris, especially late in September, Antonia chose a gown of heavy satin.

It had a short jacket fastening into the waist and was trimmed with a collar of ermine, with the same fur on the cuffs.

She washed her hair and was appalled at the amount of dust it had accumulated on the ride and from sleeping in the hay in the barn.

While she had a little difficulty in arranging it when it was surmounted by one of Worth's *chic* little hats, she looked very fashionable and very un-English.

She knew when she went on deck that the Captain and the crew looked at her in undisguised admiration, and she only hoped the same expression would be echoed in the Duke's eyes.

He was standing near the gangway, exceedingly smart and looking as if he had undertaken nothing more strenuous than a ride in the Park.

Antonia found it hard to look at him.

Now that they were back to normal life and there was no danger, no urgency, she felt as if they were drifting apart.

She wanted to cling on to him and beg him not to leave her.

"I love you. I love you," she wanted to cry, but instead with a commendable control, she said:

"Good morning, Your Grace. It is delightful to be home."

"Are you ready to go for a drive?" he asked.

"A drive?" she questioned. "I thought we should be taking the train to London."

"We are not going to London," he replied. "Not unless you particularly wish to do so."

She waited for him to explain and he went on:

"I have a cousin, the Earl of Manfred, who lives near Southampton. I have already called at his house to find that he and his wife are in Scotland. I have therefore arranged with his Secretary, who is in charge, that we shall stay there for a few days. I think we have both done enough travelling for the moment."

He smiled at Antonia as he spoke and she felt her heart turn over in her breast with excitement.

She was not to lose him immediately! He was not in such a hurry as she had feared to see the Marchioness again.

They would be together and she could not imagine anything that would be more wonderful.

The Earl's house was only a few miles outside Southampton and the Duke drove her there in the smart Phaeton which he explained also belonged to his cousin and which was drawn by two horses.

Antonia had to exclaim in delight at the sight of them. Then she said:

"Perhaps they only appear so superbly well-bred after the two which carried us from Paris."

Then she added quickly:

"Do not think I am disparaging their wonderful performance in bringing us to safety. I only wish we could have explained to them how grateful we were."

"I gave them to the man who owns the local Livery Stables," the Duke said. "I also gave him quite a considerable sum for their keep, on condition he rested them for at least a week. I think he will appreciate their worth."

"That was generous of you," Antonia said gratefully.

"I do not think either of us will forget that ride or the horses that carried us," he said quietly.

'I could never forget it,' Antonia said in her heart. 'We were alone . . . he was with me both by day and by night . . . for perhaps the last time!'

The house belonging to the Earl of Manfred was impressively Georgian with a delightful garden.

There was a staff of well-trained servants and Antonia was shown into a large, elegantly furnished bedroom which compared favourably with the State-Rooms at Doncaster Park.

There was a canopied and curtained bed in a rose pink that she thought was particularly becoming to herself. Only she remembered that the colour was of no importance as she would be sleeping alone!

The last two nights she had slept beside the Duke her body had been touching his and the first night she had held him in her arms.

"That will never happen again," she told herself miserably.

Suddenly the fact that they were back in civilisation swept over her with a feeling of despair! Now she would lose him!

She had had him to herself for so long that she could hardly remember what it was like before he had been there. To the exclusion of all else, she had concentrated all her thoughts and her feelings and love on him.

Yet she had promised him when he had asked her to marry him that she would be unobtrusive and would make no demands upon him. Now she must keep her promise.

'I cannot imagine anything more humiliating,' she thought, 'if he realises that I love him and he had to make it clear to me that he is not interested.'

What was more, she thought, such knowledge might make him feel uncomfortable, perhaps embarrassed, in which case she might see even less of him than she would do otherwise.

"I have to be very sensible, and very brave about this," she told herself, but was near to tears.

She forced herself to take an interest in her trunks, which had been brought to the house by Tour and had followed them from Southampton in a travelling-carriage also provided by the Earl's staff.

Before she had left the yacht, Antonia had remembered to ask about the Duke's clothes.

She learnt that he always had an extra wardrobe kept aboard the yacht in case he wished to embark at a moment's notice without the necessity of waiting for a valet to pack for him.

He was therefore looking resplendent and just as elegant as on their wedding-night, when Antonia entered the Salon before dinner.

The sun was sinking and the crimson-and-gold sky cast a warm glow into the long room with its French windows opening out onto a balustraded terrace.

Antonia stood just inside the door, her eyes seeking the Duke's, and for a moment it was hard to move forward.

She had spent a long time choosing what she would wear, changing her mind a dozen times.

Finally she had let the maids dress her in a gown of cardinal red which made her skin seem almost translucent.

It was, however, not a heavy gown, despite the depth of colour.

It was ornamented with the soft tulle, expensive satin ribbons, frills, and fringes which Worth had made fashionable. They accentuated the perfect curves of Antonia's figure and gave her an alluring femininity that was unmistakable.

Slowly she walked towards the Duke.

"These surroundings are somewhat different from our lodgings last night," he said with a smile, "and although I had a good luncheon I am still hungry."

His eyes were on her face as he spoke, and she had the feeling that he was talking as if he had to bridge a certain awkwardness which lay between them. But what it was she did not know.

Then as he raised her hand to his lips, she wanted desperately to hold on to him because she was afraid he would vanish.

'He will leave me now that we are home,' she thought despairingly, but aloud she said:

"Tour tells me your shoulder has withstood the journey well."

"I am well," the Duke said firmly. "It is what I have waited for, for a long time, Antonia."

She looked at him enquiringly, but at that moment dinner was announced and she put her hand shyly on his arm as he led her towards the Dining-Room.

The Earl's Chef was not as skilled as the one employed by the Duke in London, but Antonia thought that never had a meal tasted more delicious.

She kept remembering how dry and hard the bread had been the last day of their journey, and how tired she had been of the pâté, which seemed less appetising every time they sampled it. The cheese too had been over-ripe from being carried in the saddle-bag.

She thought now that the fish, fresh from the sea, the beef, from the Earl's own herd, and the pigeons, roasted until they were exactly the right tenderness, were an epicurean feast.

The Duke insisted that she should drink a little champagne.

"It will take away the last vestige of tiredness," he said.

The Duke had found out the latest news from France and he told her that Strassbourg had surrendered after a gallant defence, following the bombardment which had destroyed the magnificent old Library and killed many civilians.

"War is such a waste!" Antonia exclaimed. "It destroys not only people but also history."

"That is true," the Duke agreed, "and it seems incredible that the French should have gone to war without finding out more accurately the strength of the German Armies."

"I suppose the Prussians are very pleased at the way things are going," Antonia said in a low voice.

"Cock-a-hoop!" the Duke replied. "And I am quite certain they will extract every possible ounce of humiliation from the French."

"We can only pray that Paris will be spared," Antonia said quietly, and hoped that Labby would be safe.

When dinner was over she and the Duke moved into the Salon. The sun had now sunk and it was twilight outside, with a few stars in the sky.

The candles had been lit in the Salon and the curtains were drawn in all the windows except one. Antonia stood looking out, and then drawing a deep breath she said in a very small voice:

"I have . . . something to . . . tell you."

She turned round as she spoke to walk back towards the Duke, who was standing in front of the fireplace.

A fire was lit in the grate in case, as the Butler had explained, they should feel cold, but Antonia at the moment was cold not from the temperature but because she was extremely nervous.

The Duke set down on the mantelpiece the glass of brandy he held in his hand.

"What is it?" he asked.

"It is . . . something which may make you very . . . angry," she answered, "but I . . . have to tell . . . you."

"I promised you the night we married that I would try never to be angry with you, so I cannot imagine what it can be."

"It is . . . something of which I am very . . . ashamed."

She twisted her fingers together as she trembled, and he said quietly:

"It is not like you to be afraid, Antonia."

"I am . . . afraid of making you . . . angry."

"Then I will not be."

"You have every . . . right to be," she said miserably.

There was silence and after a moment the Duke prompted:

"I am waiting to receive this momentous confession."

His voice sounded almost apprehensive but for a moment Antonia thought she was struck dumb and would never be able to speak again.

"It is my . . . fault that you ever had to . . . fight the . . . duel."

The words came out with a rush and as she looked up at him for a fleeting second he saw the stricken consternation in her eyes.

"I spoke without . . . thinking," she went on. "I did not know the Count was the husband of the lady you were . . . with."

And there was a little sob in her voice as she continued:

"When he asked me where you were I replied you were in the garden with a very fascinating and alluring lady . . . whom I . . . suspected of being an old . . . friend."

Antonia's voice faded away and then she added:

"How could I have been so foolish . . . so idiotic to say such a thing without . . . knowing to whom I was . . . speaking?"

There was so much self-accusation in her voice that it seemed to vibrate in the air.

The Duke gave a sigh, almost as if it was one of relief. Antonia had no idea what he might have been afraid of hearing.

"You must not blame yourself," he said quietly. "The Count would have found an excuse sooner or later to fight me, as he had always wished to do."

"You will . . . forgive . . . me?" Antonia pleaded.

"I think you have made it impossible for me not to

do so, seeing how well you nursed me," the Duke replied.

"But you might have . . . died," Antonia said. "And it would have been my . . . fault. How could I have gone on . . . living, knowing that I had . . . caused your death?"

She thought she was going to burst into tears, and having no wish to lose her self-control, she turned away to walk back to the window.

She stood there looking out into the darkness, tipping back her head a little so that the tears would not brim over and run down her cheeks.

"As we are being frank with each other," she heard the Duke saying behind her, "and because once we agreed that there would be no pretence between us, I also have something to tell you, Antonia."

There was something especially solemn in the way he spoke and she waited, digging her nails into the palms of her hands. She could guess what he was going to say to her now that they were back in England.

"What I have to tell you," the Duke said, "is that I am in love."

It was what she had expected to hear him say, but it was like a mortal blow which struck at her very heart.

Just for a moment she felt numb, and then it was an agony so intense, so violent, that it tore her apart. It was only with the greatest difficulty that she did not scream and cry out.

In a voice which did not seem to be her own, she said:

"I . . . understand, and I will . . . go to Doncaster Park, as we . . . arranged."

"Do you think you will be happy there?" the Duke asked.

It was hard to fight back tears, but a pride she did not know she possessed made Antonia reply:

"I will be . . . all right."

"Alone?"

"I shall . . . have the . . . horses."

"I thought we agreed to share them."

She did not understand and after a moment she said hesitatingly:

"You . . . mean you will want . . . some of them for the . . . Marchioness?"

"Turn round, Antonia!"

She wanted to obey him but she was afraid he would read in her face what she was feeling.

She did not move and she heard him come nearer.

"You are under some misapprehension," he said quietly. "It is not the Marchioness with whom I am in love."

"Not the Marchioness?"

Now Antonia was surprised into turning round and she found he was nearer than she had thought. After one quick glance at him she looked away.

"But I . . . thought . . ." she said hesitatingly.

"So did I, for a short time," the Duke said, "but I was mistaken."

'Then there is someone else!' Antonia thought, and wondered desperately who it could be.

She could not believe it was the Comtesse, after the way her husband had behaved during the duel.

"The person I am in love with," the Duke said very quietly and slowly, as if he was choosing his words, "is someone who I think loves me as she might love a child. What I wish to find out, Antonia, is whether she loves me as a man."

It was difficult for Antonia to breathe!

Something strange had happened to her throat, and something wild and wonderful that she dared not acknowledge was rising in her breast.

"Do . . . you . . . mean. . . ?" she tried to say.

"I love someone," the Duke said very softly, "who held me in her arms and talked to me in the voice of love and who kissed my cheek and my forehead."

Antonia made a little inarticulate murmur, and then instinctively she moved towards him and hid her face against his shoulder.

His arms went round her, holding her very close.

"Can you love me as a man, my precious one?" he

asked. "I am so afraid that I might lose you now that I am well again."

He felt her quiver against him and then very gently he put his fingers under her chin and turned her face up to his.

"You kissed me, my darling," he said. "It is only fair that I should now be allowed to kiss you."

His lips were on hers and she felt a strange and wonderful thrill streak through her whole body. It was like no feeling she had ever known before, and yet it was a part of the love that she had already given him.

It was so perfect, so rapturous, so overwhelming that she thought no-one could feel such an emotion and not die of sheer happiness.

He kissed her until the room disappeared and they were alone, as she had thought they had been in Paris, on a secret island where there was no-one except themselves.

Only now it was so marvellous, so divine, that she felt she must be dreaming and this could have no substance or reality.

It was only when he raised his head to look down into her eyes and saw the wonder in them did he say tenderly:

"Now tell me how you love me."

"I . . . love you. Oh, Athol, I love . . . you with all of . . . me . . . as I have loved you, I know now . . . from the very first."

"My brave, wonderful, uncomplaining little wife," he said. "How could I know that there was any woman who could be so perfect and at the same time so courageous."

"I was never . . . afraid because I was with . . . you," Antonia murmured.

"As you always will be," he answered.

His arms tightened round her as he said:

"There are so many things for us to do together, and I think for the moment we neither of us have any wish to be in London, to be fashionable, or to clutter our house with friends."

Antonia felt that he was thinking of the Marchioness and she whispered:

"You will not be . . . bored in the country?"

"I should never be bored anywhere with you," he answered. "But we must not forget our horses! We will school them for the Steeplechase and win the prizes together. I think that will keep us fully occupied for the moment."

His lips sought hers before she could reply and now his kisses were demanding, insistent, and very passionate.

They made her feel as if her whole being dissolved into his and yet there was a fire beneath the warm wonder of them, and she surrendered herself to him, feeling that they were one and completely indivisible.

"I love you," he said later, a little unsteadily. "I love everything about you, not only your exquisite body, and your eyes which are as fascinating as looking into a crystal ball."

He kissed them before he continued:

"But I love the music of your voice, the softness of your hands, your sweetness, gentleness, and compassion."

His voice deepened as he went on:

"I never realised before that those were the things I wanted from a woman but which I knew were always missing."

"I have been so . . . jealous of the . . . Marchioness," Antonia whispered.

"Not half as jealous as I have been of that damned journalist who was making love to you when I was too ill to do so myself!"

Antonia looked at him in surprise.

"You were . . . jealous?"

"Crazily so!" the Duke replied harshly. "And I promise you, my darling, if I find other men looking at you as he did I shall be fighting not one duel but hundreds!"

"Oh, no! That I could never allow," Antonia exclaimed. "I could never go through that anxiety and misery again, thinking that it was I who had nearly killed you and that if you knew the truth you would never . . . forgive me."

"I have to forgive you."

"Why?"

"Because I realise now I cannot live without you," the Duke answered. "I want you, Antonia, because you are mine, because we belong to each other."

The fierce passion in his voice made her hide her head against his shoulder.

"I thought," she said after a moment, "that when . . . we came back to . . . England you would leave . . . me to go to the . . . Marchioness, and then . . . I was . . . going to ask . . . you . . ."

She paused and the Duke prompted:

"What were you going to ask me?"

"If you . . . would give me . . . a baby . . . because he would be . . . part of . . . you, and I would . . . have something to . . . love," she whispered.

The Duke held her so tightly she could hardly breathe.

"I will give you a baby, Antonia, but only if you promise me one thing."

"What is . . . that?" she asked a little apprehensively.

"That you will not love it more than you love me," he answered. "I am prepared to share a small part of you with our children, but only so long as you love me best. That you hold me in your arms as you held me when I was ill, and make me sure that I never need be afraid of losing you or of being hurt."

Antonia's eyes seemed to hold all the stars in the sky as she looked up at him.

He knew that while she had never been really beautiful before, love had made her lovelier than any woman he had ever known.

"Do you promise?" he asked, his lips very close to hers.

"I promise to . . . love you always and for . . . ever," she answered, "more than . . . anything else in the world or . . . in Heaven. I am yours completely and . . . absolutely yours, my darling, and I adore you."

The last words were lost against the Duke's lips as he carried her once again away to their secret island where there were only themselves and no-one else could ever encroach.

ABOUT THE AUTHOR

BARBARA CARTLAND, the celebrated romantic author, historian, playwright, lecturer, political speaker and television personality, has now written over 150 books, Miss Cartland has had a number of historical books published and several biographical ones, including that of her brother, Major Ronald Cartland, who was the first Member of Parliament to be killed in the War. This book had a Foreword by Sir Winston Churchill.

In private life, Barbara Cartland, who is a Dame of the Order of St. John of Jerusalem, has fought for better conditions and salaries for Midwives and nurses. As President of the Royal College of Midwives (Hertfordshire Branch), she has been invested with the first Badge of Office ever given in Great Britain, which was subscribed to by the Midwives themselves. She has also championed the cause for old people and founded the first Romany Gypsy Camp in the world.

Barbara Cartland is deeply interested in Vitamin Therapy and is President of the British National Association for Health.

Barbara Cartland

The world's bestselling author of romantic fiction. Her stories are always captivating tales of intrigue, adventure and love.

☐	A VERY NAUGHTY ANGEL	2107	$1.25
☐	THE CRUEL COUNT	2128	$1.25
☐	CALL OF THE HEART	2140	$1.25
☐	AS EAGLES FLY	2147	$1.25
☐	THE MASK OF LOVE	2366	$1.25
☐	AN ARROW OF LOVE	2426	$1.25
☐	A GAMBLE WITH HEARTS	2430	$1.25
☐	A KISS FOR THE KING	2433	$1.25
☐	A FRAME OF DREAMS	2434	$1.25
☐	THE FRAGRANT FLOWER	2435	$1.25
☐	MOON OVER EDEN	2437	$1.25
☐	THE GOLDEN ILLUSION	2449	$1.25
☐	FIRE ON THE SNOW	2450	$1.25
☐	THE HUSBAND HUNTERS	2461	$1.25
☐	THE SHADOW OF SIN	6430	$1.25
☐	SAY YES, SAMANTHA	7834	$1.25
☐	THE KARMA OF LOVE	8106	$1.25
☐	BEWITCHED	8630	$1.25
☐	THE IMPETUOUS DUCHESS	8705	$1.25

Buy them at your local bookseller or use this handy coupon: